One Wrong Summer

JULIA BODWELL

ISBN: 9798435977035

Cover design by: GRAPHIKLEE

DEDICATION

To you, reader, for taking a chance on Janelle.

Monday, September 13th
Fall of Freshman Year

It's been thirty-six days, twenty-two hours, eleven minutes and eight seconds since the worst day of my life.

Despite the distance that every second creates, it feels like yesterday, the memory still fresh in my mind even as I try so desperately to forget. I shudder at the thought of it, swallowing a scream that bubbles up in my chest as I simultaneously swallow down a spoonful of cereal.

I continue shoveling my breakfast into my mouth, my eyes glued to my phone's screen even as my mind reels, refusing to look away from Jason's most recent Instagram post. The longer I stare at the picture, a selfie of Jason and Bethany kissing at the skatepark, the harder my heart thumps against the inside of my chest. Seeing him this happy without me is nauseating, but it's like a car accident; I can't tear my eyes away no matter how bad it makes me feel inside.

Besides, the pain of seeing him with her is still a thousand times less agonizing than it would be if he knew the truth.

You got what you deserved.

"Janelle, the bus will be here in ten," my mom says, interrupting my thoughts as she glides into the kitchen. She grabs a seltzer from the fridge, her perfectly manicured French tips clinking lightly against the aluminum, before floating out of the room again.

Nine minutes and forty-one seconds, I silently correct her, glancing at the clock above the sink. As I watch her go, her knee-length skirt rippling behind her in the imaginary wake of her power walk, I miss my mouth with the spoon and dribble almond milk onto the shiny granite countertop. I wipe it away with the sleeve of my shirt and go back to my phone, my insides turning as I continue to overanalyze Jason's picture. The Raisin Bran in my stomach threatens to come back up as I read through the picture's comments.

Such a hot couple!

U guys r so cute 2gether!

Adorbs

Good 4 u, bro

Nice upgrade!

I swallow back another scream working its way up my throat and swipe out of the app, setting my phone face down on the counter. Forcing a few deep breaths and counting silently to ten, I try to push away the thought that's creeping back into my mind, the only thought I've had for the last five days, six hours, nineteen minutes and four seconds since Jason posted that photo, the same thought I've tried to silence for the last thirty-six days, twenty-two hours, thirteen minutes, and twenty-one seconds:

This is all your fault.

Monday, September 13th
Fall of Freshman Year

When the number 11 bus finally picks me up, I slump into a seat at the back, stuffing earbuds in and staring out the window. As I let the music quiet the noise in my brain, I settle back into my seat, watching the trees as they blur by, melting into one giant blob of color as the bus rockets me closer and closer to its final destination.

After a twenty-two minute and forty-three second drive, the bus dumps me at the school's main entrance. I shuffle my way off, falling into step with the hordes of other miserable-looking teens marching their way into what will feel like prison for the next six to eight hours (give or take extracurriculars). I scuttle along down the sidewalk to the front doors, grateful just to hide among the crowd entering the building.

As I trudge through the hallways, I keep my eyes on the feet of everyone around me and try to navigate through the sea of students inconspicuously. If I keep my head down, hopefully I won't run into Jason or Bethany, or any of their couple friends, even though those couple friends used to be *my* friends once upon a time.

Your fault.

I round the corner and head towards the safety of Ms. Sharp's classroom, pushing the dark thoughts back down. As I walk closer, I watch as she lingers near the door, smiling and greeting students as they pass her in the hall. I wait for her to be distracted with another student before I slip quickly into the room unnoticed.

As usual, I'm one of the first students to arrive, eager to avoid socializing in the halls before the bell rings. I pick a desk in the back corner, near the window, the same one I've sat in every morning since school started. My foot starts bouncing as I eyeball the door, willing every student that walks through it to be either Shelley, Crystal, or both. The clock tells me to shut up, that they still have ten minutes and fourteen seconds to get here.

I dig a paper clip out of my backpack and scratch aimlessly at the corner of my binder, hoping no one sits in the two vacant seats on either side of me. I hear Ms. Sharp laughing with someone at the door and I glance up to see Shelley; she spots me and gives me a small wave, heading my way.

"What's up, buttercup?" She plops down at the desk next to me, glancing down at the *J-A-S-* I've successfully carved into my binder without realizing it.

"Really, Nell?" she questions, raising an eyebrow at me. "This isn't a Lifetime drama." She flicks her perfectly straightened blonde hair out of her face. "Plus, *you* broke up with *him*, remember? You don't exactly have the right to play the scorned lover after dumping him without so much as an explanation."

If only you knew the reason why, I can't help but think.

She opens her backpack and pulls out her planner and pencil case. I keep scratching with intention now, finishing the *O-* and the *N-* to make the word complete as she pulls out eight gel pens, one for each color of the ROYGBIV spectrum, plus black. She lines them up along the edge of her desk and positions her planner right underneath them.

I look down at my binder, second-guessing the word I've etched there, staring up at me like a threat. I scratch it out until it becomes illegible, then toss the paper clip back into my bag.

"Just because we broke up doesn't mean I want him dating my friend," I grumble, flicking bits of binder off my desk. "It's called girl code."

I regret my words immediately, knowing what I did was a thousand times worse. I swallow back my unease and wait for Shelley to push for more, my heart racing at the thought of telling her the truth, almost deciding it would be worth it to finally tell someone, anyone. But, after weeks of prying to get the answer out of me, she seems to have finally given up and lost interest. She gives me a closed-mouth smirk instead, eyebrows scrunched high in disapproval, before opening her planner.

With nothing else to say, I open the binder to my geometry section and stare down at the unfinished problems on the page. The warning bell rings. I glance up at the clock, watching the seconds tick by and wondering where Crystal is.

If she doesn't get here in four minutes and thirty-one seconds, she's going to be late.

Shelley notices me watching the clock. "She's going to be late today," she says, reading my mind. "Doctor's appointment. She won't be in til third."

Why didn't she tell me *that?* I wonder. Ever since school started, things have felt off, as if the breakup wasn't just between Jason and me. I shrug away the thought, knowing exactly where it leads.

Shelley has her planner open now, and is busy color coding her class schedule, as well as all the homework assignments that are due this week. When the bell finally rings to start class, I dig a pencil out of my backpack and continue working on the equations in front of me.

"You know, if you spent half as much time actually *doing* your homework as you do writing it down, you might have better grades," I mumble, side eyeing her planner.

"I'm perfectly happy with my B-minus average, thank you very much," she retorts. "Not everyone wants to be an overachiever A-plus student like you, y'know. There's more to life than just school. And why are you taking tenth grade math, anyway?" she questions, gesturing to my notebook. "You've basically guaranteed we'll never be in the same math class again."

I can feel her gaze on the side of my face as she waits for an explanation, but like so many other questions in my life right now, I ignore it and let this one go unanswered, too. Even if I found the right words, she wouldn't understand that the only reason I elected to take Geometry this year instead of waiting until next year like everyone else was because I needed something that would serve as a distraction from all the painful memories of the last month and a half. If I told her that the only problems in my life I seem to have any control over solving these days originate from my math textbook, she would sigh and call me melodramatic.

Or worse, ask me if I'm okay.

I'm not.

But she doesn't need to know that.

Like every day since *that* day, silence seems to be easier, and safer, so instead of having a real conversation with my oldest friend, I swallow back the words that threaten to escape from my lips and give her a half-hearted shrug. Then I tuck my long, brown hair behind my ears and allow the math problems in front of me to carry me away from my real problems, if only for a little while.

*****

Just like every other day since the first day of school, I've managed to make it through my first four class periods without any Jason and Bethany sightings. I've even managed to keep myself busy enough with schoolwork to keep my mind from wandering back to that August night.

But when the bell rings for lunch, my stomach sinks as I realize the dreaded reality I've been trying to avoid all day has arrived once again.

I pack my things slowly, stuffing my notebook into my black Jansport backpack, slipping my worn copy of Romeo and Juliet in after.

"When does this story start to pick up?" Tyler asks from beside me as he shuffles his own class materials into his camo messenger bag.

I turn and glance up at him, meeting his blue eyes with my brown ones and giving him a half-smile and a shrug.

"You have to remember Shakespeare isn't like modern stories," I start.

Tyler rolls his eyes and puts his hands up, palms towards me to stop me. "Sorry, I forgot who I was talking to," he says, jokingly. "Shouldn't have asked."

I force a small laugh, trying to shrug his comment off and not take it personal, reminding myself that most teenagers *don't* read Shakespeare in their spare time for fun.

"Janelle, guess what?" Brendan singsongs into my ear, interrupting my thoughts as he comes bounding over. "It's cheesesteak day!" He slings his arm around my shoulder, hustling me out the door before I can respond.

"I don't understand how you guys can eat that," Dougie chimes in, falling into step next to Tyler as we make our way down the hall. "It's basically plastic cheese that's been liquefied."

"Don't knock it 'til you try it," Brendan replies.

I slow and turn back for Shelley, but she catches my eye before I can speak.

"Bathroom," she mouths by way of explanation, and makes a sharp turn towards the girl's room.

Disappointed, I let Brendan and the others whisk me away to the cafeteria, towards what used to be my favorite school lunch, back when we were in middle school. Back when food still tasted like food.

As we enter the brightly lit cafeteria, I spot Jason and Bethany across the room. I avert my gaze, keeping my eyes fixed on Brendan's back as we make our way to what's become our usual spot, a rectangular table by a large bay of windows overlooking the courtyard. I watch longingly through the floor-to-ceiling windows as juniors and seniors mill about the courtyard, lounging on the picnic tables and in the grass, enjoying their upperclassmen privileges. I'd give anything to be out in the fresh air with them, away from the stifling humiliation of seeing my ex-boyfriend with one of my friends.

Former friend, I remind myself.

Your fault, I also remind myself.

Without the ability to run from the room, the best I can do is keep them out of sight, so I sling my bag down on a chair facing the windows, keeping my back to Jason and Bethany's table. Dougie and Tyler slide in on the opposite side next to Crystal, who's already digging into her salami and cheese sandwich.

"Hey, you made it," I breathe at her.

She gives me a closed-mouth smile as she chews the bite of food in her mouth, two perfect dimples appearing in each of her ebony cheeks.

"No Petey today?" Tyler asks her.

"No," she swallows and says. "He had a migraine when he woke up."

Though Crystal's new boyfriend is now a permanent part of our friend group, I hadn't even noticed he was missing. Which, I suppose is a good thing, since our group dynamic doesn't seem to change whether he's there or not. Now that Jason and I aren't together anymore, Crystal's the only one in our group who's dating someone and I realize with a pang of guilt I liked it better when I was the one in a relationship.

Is this what she felt like when I was the one with the boyfriend?

"Nell, shall we?" Brendan asks, pulling me out of my thoughts. He gestures towards the lunch line, which is starting to curve out of the gated food serving area and into the main lunchroom.

"See, we aren't the only ones who love cheesesteak day," I turn to Dougie and smirk, more for Brendan's sake than my own.

"Whatever. You'll never convince me," Dougie replies, turning his nose up at us. Brendan cackles and grabs my elbow, steering me away from the table.

The line has gotten so long it's now backed up halfway into the lunchroom. I feel my insides tighten as Brendan and I quickly slip into line behind two guys in football jerseys, closer to Jason's table than is comfortable. I put every ounce of energy into keeping my gaze fixed straight ahead, telling myself over and over to keep staring forward.

"You okay?" Brendan asks, oblivious to my agony.

"Mmhmm," I grunt, eyes forward.

"Good. I need you 100% for practice this afternoon. I know it's only been a few weeks, but we've *got* to knock Dougie off that high horse of his. Shouldn't be hard for you to do. You're the team's *MVP,* after all," he adds sarcastically, wiggling his fingers at me.

"Still bitter that I'm a better chess player, huh?" I reply, flicking him on the shoulder.

As the line moves forward, we shuffle our way into the safety of the food serving area, each step bringing me further and further away from Jason. Brendan passes me a plastic tray and we slide along the glass case of options, each grabbing a steaming cheesesteak and a plate of French fries. I add a bottle of water to my tray and Brendan adds an orange Gatorade to his.

We make our way to the checkout line, squeezing in next to a short kid with a tall, red mohawk. His hair blocks most of my view of the cafeteria, but as he bends forward to browse the chip display, I see them.

Planting small, playful kisses on each other's lips. Staring deep into each other's eyes. His hands twirling a piece of her curly blonde hair. Her hands smoothing his soft, brown locks back behind his lopsided ears.

My heart stops for a moment as I watch them, totally lost in each other. When Bethany pulls away and goes back to her lunch, Jason looks up, his green eyes locking onto mine from across the room. I feel my hands tremble, feel the tray I'm holding get heavy, my fingers growing slick with sweat. I don't even realize I've dropped the tray and everything on it until I feel Brendan's hand on my shoulder.

"Janelle? Are you alright?" he asks.

The kid with the mohawk has turned around, is helping Brendan swipe as much of the debris back onto my tray as they can while I stand there, frozen. A lunch lady has appeared with a mop, is pushing the globby cheese around on the floor, trying to clean it up.

I shake my head to stop the ringing in my ears. I find Jason in the crowd again, but he's gone back to his lunch, distracted by something one of his friends is saying.

"I-I'm sorry," I stutter, "I'm not feeling well all of a sudden." I quickly push my way past Brendan, past the kid with the mohawk and the other students who've stopped to watch the commotion, back out into the main lunchroom. I walk swiftly back towards our table, snatching my bag off my chair as I continue pushing on towards the exit doors.

"Janelle?" I hear Tyler's voice as I whirl past, but it's soft and muted, like being underwater. I don't stop to explain, knowing if I can just make it out into the hallway without breaking down even more, without Jason seeing me totally lose it, things might be okay.

I push through the double doors of the cafeteria and make my way down the hall to the front office, shuffling up to the secretary's desk.

"Yes, dear?" the woman behind the desk asks. She pushes her frameless glasses up onto her head and looks up at me from her swivel chair.

"Um, I'm not feeling very well," I tell her, glad it isn't a total lie.

She asks a few more questions before retrieving the nurse, who brings me back to a small, sterile room with a cot.

"Go ahead and lie down," the nurse tells me, pointing to the cot. "I'll bring you some water." She leaves the room and I slump onto the cot, the brown blanket that covers it scratchy and uncomfortable, but I don't even care, so long as I'm out of the cafeteria and away from Jason, away from that look he gave me.

As I wait for the nurse to return, I watch the clock on the wall, watch the second-hand as it *tick tick ticks* by, counting the minutes left until I can go home and release the scream that's building inside me. Ninety-seven minutes and thirty-four seconds until the last bell of the day will ring. Ninety-seven minutes and thirty-three seconds until one more day of school has passed. Ninety-seven minutes and thirty-two seconds until I can stop pretending I'm the same Janelle I used to be. Ninety-seven minutes and thirty-one seconds until I'm another day further from the worst day of my life.

Tuesday, August 7th
Summer Before Freshman Year

"We gonna talk about what just happened?" Lauren asked as Janelle slowly tiptoed up the front porch steps. Janelle froze mid-step, unaware her sister was lingering in the dark, waiting for her.

Could she possibly know what had transpired in the mere hours since they'd parted ways on the beach?

Lauren stopped rocking in the chair by the front door of their beach house, waiting for her sister's reply. Her arms were crossed tightly over her chest, her thin lips drawn into an even thinner line, her perfectly manicured eyebrows knitted in fury.

"There's nothing to talk about," Janelle said, sweat beading under her armpits. "Nothing happened." Her stomach turned, not from the alcohol, but from the lie that so easily slipped from her lips.

It was the first lie she'd ever told her sister.

"*Really*," Lauren continued, standing and blocking Janelle's path to the door. "So you *didn't* just get shitfaced and completely humiliate both of us, then?"

Janelle sighed with relief, glad her sister couldn't see the truth written on her face. "So I got drunk, what's the big deal? It's not like *you've* never gotten drunk behind Mom and Dad's back." Even among the shadows, she could see her sister's face blanch at the rebuttal, momentarily thrown off-guard.

"Just let it go, okay?" she continued, using the moment to her advantage. "*Please*, Lauren?"

"Fine," Lauren replied tersely, her face softening slightly as the fight melted out of her. "But don't you *ever* put me in that position again, you hear?"

"Yes. Of course," Janelle nodded, eager to move on and put this night behind her.

"And whatever you do, don't mention this to Mom and Dad. They'd kill me if they found out I left you there by yourself." Lauren's eyes widened as she thought of the punishment her parents would serve her if they ever found out she'd abandoned her younger sister on a foreign beach with strangers.

"I won't, I promise," Janelle assured her sister, thinking of her own punishment as she followed her older sister into the darkened house.

With one last look back out into the night, Janelle quietly latched the door behind her, her thoughts drowning out the thumping of her heart.

I never want to think of this night ever again.

Tuesday, September 14th
Fall of Freshman Year

"How you doin' after yesterday?" Brendan asks me the next day in English class. He's perched on a stool next to my desk as we diagram compound-complex sentences.

"I'm good," I lie. "Just felt a bit woozy all of a sudden." My eyes drift from my paper across the room to where Shelley and her group work on their own handouts, wondering when she'll bother to ask how I'm doing.

If she'll even ask at all.

"Well, I'm glad you're okay," Brendan goes on, interrupting my thoughts. "You looked like you'd seen a ghost."

"Or like you might throw up," Tyler chimes in. His dark, bushy eyebrows scrunch up in confusion as he stares down at his paper. "What the hell is a prepositional phrase, anyway?" he grumbles, leaning across his desk to get a better look at my paper.

"It's a group of words consisting of a preposition, its object, and any modifiers," I tell him.

He stares at me blankly, his blue eyes growing wide.

"It modifies a verb or a noun," I elaborate.

"If you say so," he shrugs, and goes back to scribbling on his paper.

"So did you?" Brendan asks me.

"Did I what?"

"Y'know. Pass out. Throw up. See a ghost. Et cetera." He looks at me unblinkingly, waiting for a reply.

"No," I say. "I guess I was just lightheaded and needed to lay down for a bit. The nurse gave me some water and let me rest."

"On those itchy cots?" Tyler asks. "Those things are the worst."

Before I can agree with him, the bell rings and our English teacher, Mr. Vogel, clears his throat over the noise of shuffling papers.

"Any work not finished in class needs to be completed as homework," he reminds us as everyone begins packing up. I write my name on the top of my handout and walk it over to his desk, dropping it in the turn-in tray next to his laptop.

"Excellent, Janelle," he tells me with a smile. "I look forward to grading your work."

I give him a shy smile just as Courtney Navid comes up and deposits her paper on top of mine, giving Mr. Vogel a megawatt smile and waiting for her own compliment.

"You, too, Courtney," he tells her. Her fake smile drops and she all but stomps off to her desk. I scurry back to my own desk, where Tyler has pulled his away from mine back into its normal position, two feet of space between us.

"I thought we would finish together, Nell," he whines.

"Don't worry, I'll still help you," I assure him.

"*Thank* you," he says, drawing out the word *'thank'* in obvious relief.

I sling my backpack over one shoulder, heading to the door to wait for my friends.

"Well that assignment was a doozy," Dougie says when he reaches us, pushing his black-framed glasses further up on his nose.

"Tell me about it," Brendan agrees.

I don't mention how easy the assignment was for me, instead keeping quiet as we all start off down the hallway to lunch.

I sense Shelley stop behind us and I turn back towards her.

"You coming?" I ask.

She bites her lip, looking uncomfortably around the hallway.

"Yeah, I'll be right behind you," she finally says, not making a move to join me.

"Okay," I reply uneasily, finally turning down the hall to catch up with the guys, leaving her lingering at the classroom door.

Weird, I can't help but think.

When we arrive at our lunch table, Crystal is already there, munching a peanut butter and banana sandwich, her boyfriend, Petey, at her left side carving some sort of hieroglyphic into the table.

"Hi guys," she says as we walk up, smoothing her braids back from her face.

"Hey Crystal," Tyler says as he slumps into the chair across from her, leaning across the table to bump fists with Petey. "S'up Collins?" he asks. In his typical non-verbal fashion, Petey makes a gesture to acknowledge Tyler's question, this time a peace sign, then goes back to his carving.

"Where's Shell?" Crystal asks as I slide into the chair on Tyler's right. I scoot myself in close to the table, keeping my back firmly facing the direction of Jason's table. I can't afford to have another episode, not two days in a row.

"She said she'd catch up," I reply, wondering what she's really up to.

"There she is now," Dougie says as he settles into the seat next to Crystal's. He points his chin in the direction of the door, his hands working hard to unscrew a metal canister of soup. I turn just as Shelley, Bethany, and Jason walk in together. The girls say something to each other and share a quick hug before parting ways, Bethany and Jason making their way to the opposite side of the room as Shelley makes her way towards us.

"Hey," she says as she joins the table. She doesn't make eye contact with me as she sits next to Dougie, pulling a Slim Fast shake from her Juicy Couture backpack.

"Friending with the enemy, Shell?" Brendan asks before chomping down on a shiny, red apple. He knits his red eyebrows in disgust as he chews, waiting for Shelley's reply.

"Last I checked, Bethany and I were still friends. Plus, *Nell* was the dumper, not the dumpee, so why's everyone making this such a big deal?" she questions, still refusing to look at me.

"Still feels like a betrayal," Dougie counters. I'm unsure if he's referring to Bethany's behavior, or Shelley's.

"It's not like Bethany swooped in and stole Nell's boyfriend. She gave him up willingly,"

Shelley goes on, trying hard to convince us all. "You just need to find a new guy to occupy your time," she says, finally turning to me. "It would make your life so much better."

"Janelle doesn't need a boyfriend to make her worth something," Brendan cuts in before I can say anything. Instead, I pull the edges of my ham and cheese sandwich apart.

"Well, it certainly helps pass the time," Shelley replies. "Right, Crys?"

"What?" she says, mid-bite.

"Nevermind," Shelley says, waving her off. "All I meant was maybe it's time to let it go and move on. You sure seemed ready to do that the day you dumped him, anyway." She stares hard at me, boring into me with her almond-colored eyes.

"Yeah," I grumble, breaking eye contact and going back to my pile of crust. I mush the pieces together into a bread ball, wondering if maybe Shelley's right. Maybe it *is* time to let go and move on.

In fact, I'd love nothing more than to forget any of this ever happened in the first place.

Thursday, September 16th
Fall of Freshman Year

During 4th period, I find my mind drifting from Romeo and Juliet to what Shelley said at lunch on Tuesday. After almost literally running into Jason and Bethany holding hands in the hallway yesterday, I guess I *could* use a real distraction right about now, something that will consume me more than just difficult math problems and extra credit reading assignments.

While I don't agree that a new boyfriend will solve any of my problems, maybe it wouldn't hurt to have someone new and different to occupy my time, or at least occupy my thoughts. I'd take any and all distractions right now if it keeps my mind from thinking about Jason, and our breakup, and that night.

"Janelle, let's be in a group." Tyler leans over his desk and whispers, snapping me out of my thoughts.

"Huh?" I turn to him, visibly confused.

He flicks me playfully in the arm. "For the reenactment scene. Y'know, the one Vogel just assigned moments ago?" He arches his bushy eyebrows as he tries to figure out where my mind was at.

"Right," I blink and nod in agreement. "Of course. The usual gang?" I ask, looking towards the rest of our friends in their assigned seats across the room.

"Duh," Tyler replies.

Shelley is staring back at me, giving me a glaring look that says *'we better be in the same group, or else.'* I give her, as well as Brendan and Dougie, a nod with my chin, nonverbally inviting them across the room to join us. As everyone in the room shuffles into their groups, I pray this assignment will go smoothly, no stranger to the tension that started between Brendan and Shelley right around the same time my world began collapsing in on itself, escalating ever since. I swallow back my anxiety and plaster a smile on my face, ready to get to work and drown out my thoughts.

"Okay, so we've decided on the scene, what about roles?" Brendan asks seven minutes and two seconds later.

"I am *not* dying in this scene," Shelley whines as she examines her cuticles.

"Oh-*kay*," Brendan says, drawing out the word. "Super helpful, considering two people have to die in this scene. Anyone else?" I can tell by the way his nostrils are flaring that he's growing more and more annoyed.

"I'll be Mercutio?" I say, more of a question, willing to take any role at this point to keep things from escalating. "I don't mind dying."

"Awesome, Nell," Brendan says, flashing me a toothy grin and jotting my name down on the character sheet. "I feel like I should be Romeo, then."

"Really," Shelley snorts. "What makes you think that?"

Brendan ignores her comment, and the accompanying smirk she's giving him, jotting his own name down next to Romeo's.

"I don't mind dying, either," Dougie says. "Put me down for Tybalt."

"Perfect. Ty, you wanna be Benvolio?" Brendan asks, looking up from the paper. "He's the level-headed one in the scene, trying to avoid confrontation with the Capulets."

"Sure, whatever you guys want," Tyler replies, easy-going as always.

He'll make the perfect Benvolio, I think.

"So, Shelley, I guess that leaves you to be one of Tybalt's annoying cronies. You can just sort of hang out in the background and pass judgement on others. Shouldn't be too hard for you to do." Brendan gives her a look of smug satisfaction.

"Mmhmm," Shelley says, "And you would know."

"Guys," I interject, trying to diffuse what's about to become a full-blown argument. "Let's just stay focused, okay?"

"We wanna film this outside of class, right?" Dougie asks. I give him a small smile, grateful for the turn in conversation. "Nell's dad has some killer medieval swords hanging in their living room, maybe he'll let us use them!"

Brendan's face lights up at the prospect; he turns to me for agreement, but Shelley interrupts before I can say anything.

"Um, keyword being *killer*? I'm so not doing this scene if you make me use a real sword. The last thing I need is to lose a finger or two right before the fall concert." She flicks her blonde ponytail off her shoulder and purses her plump, red lips, giving the guys a disgusted look.

We all know how she's been praying to land first chair for flute this year, but this seems a bit extreme, even for her. As if losing a finger is even possible with a bunch of antique swords that probably haven't even been sharpened since they were forged from the hellfire of whatever ancient civilization they originated from. But, knowing Shelley, she won't budge until she gets her way.

"My dad probably wouldn't let us use the swords, anyway," I say. Brendan's face falls and Shelley looks triumphant. I struggle to find a way to compromise, wanting to please everyone. "At least not with an exposed blade," I go on. "But we can film at my house, and use them as props? I'm sure my dad would be okay with it, as long as we don't remove them from their protective scabbards."

"Sounds badass either way," Dougie says.

"Yeah, sounds cool," Tyler agrees.

I give Brendan and Shelley a look, hoping the compromise settles things once and for all. There are still a few grumbles from both but finally, everyone nods. Luckily, I'm saved by the bell before any more drama can start between my best girl friend and my best guy friend, who never really became actual friends themselves.

"Nell, can I talk to you for a sec?" Shelley grabs my arm as I start shoving things back into my bag. Brendan looks over at me.

"I'll meet you at lunch," I wave him on. He tightens the straps of his backpack and tousles his flaming red hair, the way I know he's uncomfortable or anxious, before finally turning to go.

"What's up?" I ask, wondering what's on her mind. Wondering why it couldn't wait until our lunchtime gossip.

"So, I know you're still not cool with Bethany and Jason dating," she starts. "Which I don't really understand, by the way, since you broke it off with Jason, so it's not like you really have a right to be mad that he's moved on, and the rest of us shouldn't have to suffer because of your bad decision-making..." She's rambling now, each word like a tiny knife jabbing into my heart.

I sling my bag over my shoulder and head for the door, not wanting to hear any more of Shelley's judgment. I stop short when I see Bethany lingering in the hallway outside, glancing our way as if she's waiting for something. As if she's waiting for Shelley.

Oh.

"But you know Bethany is still our friend, and we can't just ditch her because you're clearly still hung up on Jason for whatever reason. It's not fair that everyone else has to stop being friends just because Jason moved on after you dumped him, y'know?" She bites her lip, like what she's saying is really difficult for her.

"We?" is all I say in response.

"Me. Crystal. Petey."

"Oh."

"So we're going to sit with them for lunch here and there, just to make sure, you know, Bethany knows we're still her friend, too." She pauses a beat, searching my face for any clue as to my reaction. I give her nothing. "Don't be mad."

"I get it." I give her a weak smile, biting my tongue to keep from screaming, to stop myself from shouting the reason why I broke it off with Jason.

But as much as it might make it a little easier for Shelley to know the truth, I know deep down the truth would be harder to swallow, that it's just easier to keep it buried inside and hope no one ever finds out what I did.

"Thanks, Nell," she says, giving me a hug before sauntering off to join Bethany. I watch as they walk off, slowly counting up from one to ten and back down again before following after them.

As I drift through the hallway, my hand slips into my front jeans pocket, fingering the safety pin nestled there. I round the corner towards the cafeteria, the familiar itch weaving its way into my brain and taking over, and at the last minute, I double back and duck into the girls' bathroom.

I check the bottoms of each stall for feet before barricading myself in the last stall. The toilet has no lid, so I perch on top of the tank, resting my feet on the toilet paper dispenser. I roll up my sleeve to expose the soft, white flesh of my left wrist, the faint scars crisscrossed there slightly darker against my faded tan. I wiggle my fingers, clenching and unclenching my fist to watch as the tendons in my arm roll back and forth under my skin. The blue veins stare up at me, taunting me, daring me to do what I know I can't, what I know I won't. That isn't the point of this, after all. Instead, I scratch a shallow X across the inside of my forearm, watching as tiny beads of red spring up from the superficial cuts, hovering like drops of water pooling on my skin. I grab a piece of toilet paper, press it to the bleeding wound for a minute, and wait for my mind to feel nothing.

Monday, August 13th
Summer Before Freshman Year

Every morning since that night, Janelle woke tangled in her bed, drenched in sweat, thrashing to escape from the pile of sheets that twisted around her like a vise. The memory, still sharp in her mind only days later, was her last thought before falling asleep at night and her first thought when she woke.

That morning was no exception. She could still smell the sea salt stinging her nostrils, could still hear the crashing of waves pounding in her ears, could almost feel the grit of the sand still clinging to her slick skin.

She shook away the details and sank into her bed for a few minutes without moving, staring up at the ceiling and willing the living nightmare to end. But it didn't, and she knew it wouldn't, and so without having anything else to do but get up, she removed herself from the confines of her bedding, swiped her phone off the nightstand, and headed into the bathroom.

Janelle turned on the tap and powered her phone on, opening various social media apps as she waited for the water to warm up. As she scrolled her newsfeed, a text notification popped up on her screen, a message from Bethany. Janelle's breath caught in her throat as she read it:

Jason n I are together. Wanted u to hear it from me instead of some1 else.

She read the string of words again and again, the letters blurring as tears filled her eyes, a few escaping down her cheeks and plummeting to the tile floor like bombs. Janelle's heart sped up, banging against her chest in every effort to escape from her body.

"No," she whispered, setting her phone down on the vanity. "No, no, no, no."

It hasn't even been a week yet, and he's already moved on? her thoughts screamed.

She knew she had no right to be angry, not after what she'd done, not after how she'd treated him. But did she really mean so little to Jason that he could move on so quickly? And with her *friend,* no less?

The picture of everyone at the lake flashed in her mind, the momentary paranoia she'd felt that led to all of this becoming real in an instant. Feeling dizzy, she grabbed onto the edge of the sink to steady herself. Her breath came in ragged gasps, like she was choking, and she felt an immense pressure squeezing her, forcing the air from her lungs.

The tap still running, Janelle scooped up handfuls of water, splashing it over her face, trying to wash away her agony. But the water had turned hot, and burned her skin, suffocating her even more. She turned the water off, grabbed the hand towel from its hook, and wiped her face, biting down into the fabric as she held back a wail.

How do I make this stop? she asked herself, balling the towel up in her fist and trying to squeeze all her anger into it. *How do I make this pain stop?*

A thought entered her mind, something she remembered seeing in a movie once, something she'd never dared to consider, not until now, not until the pain from that night, and all of its repercussions, had become so intense that she thought she might burst.

An idea she never thought she'd be desperate enough to try.

She flung open bathroom drawers, digging through the assortment of hygiene products, makeup, medicine, and other random items that she and her sister kept stored in their shared bathroom, looking for anything that might get the job done.

Her fingers closed around a pair of cuticle scissors, and she yanked them free of the drawer, sliding to the tile floor in a heap. The sharp points glinted up at her from behind her tears, beckoning. Hesitantly, she pushed the sleeve of her sleepshirt up past her elbow, her right hand shaking as she lowered the edge of the scissors to the newly sun-kissed skin of her wrist. The veins beneath her skin glowed a fluorescent blue, the tendons pulled tight, taunting her. Terrified of what she was about to do, of what could go wrong, she pressed down lightly, just enough for small beads of red to spring up, following the shallow line the scissors drew up the flesh of her arm. She pressed a little harder then, deep enough for more drops of blood to leak out, not deep enough to warrant stitches.

At first, seeing the blood made her feel woozy, her head spinning a little as the gravity of the situation sank in. But as more and more droplets sprang up, she realized her mind was quieting, the ache in her arm drowning out the ache in her heart.

Spurred on by this revelation, she drew the point of the scissors further up her arm, and only when she'd just about reached the crook of her elbow did she let them drop, clattering to the floor and sprinkling flecks of red on the white tiles. She slumped against the cabinet, feeling only the throbbing in her arm and nothing else. She pressed the hand towel to her skin and closed her eyes, a small feeling of relief washing over her as she allowed the physical pain to drown out the emotional one.

Thursday, September 16th
Fall of Freshman Year

"Janelle, can you please set the table for dinner?" my mom asks later that night as she sprinkles seasoning into a frying pan of ground beef.

"I'm doing my homework, mom," I reply without looking up from my math textbook.

"You could use a break, sweetheart, you've been working on that since you got home from school." She gives me a look and I close my book, sliding off my barstool and shuffling towards the silverware drawer.

"Is Lauren coming for dinner tonight?" I ask as I set out utensils for three, hovering over the fourth spot at the table as I await a reply.

"No, she and Brett have plans. She sends her best though, and hopes to make it home next weekend." She doesn't turn around as she answers, and I know there's a look of disappointment on her face. I guess I'd be disappointed, too, if my 19-year-old daughter no longer needed me.

"Let your father know dinner is ready," she tells me. I trudge to the side door off the kitchen, opening it and peering out into the dingy garage.

"Dinner!" I shout.

"Be right there!" my dad calls back from behind his Kawasaki 450 dirt bike. The one I'm not allowed to ride, according to my mother. The one I've secretly been dreaming of riding ever since I was big enough to reach the handlebars. Not that I would ever tell my parents that.

At the sound of my voice, our chocolate Lab, Ninja, looks up from where she's lounging on the floor near my dad. It takes her a few seconds to get her feet under her, but she's finally up and on the move towards me, slowly pulling herself up each step and through the door.

"Hey, old girl," I whisper to her as I scratch the graying fur behind her ears. She responds with a panting breath, tongue hanging out of her toothless mouth in a way that makes it look like she's smiling at me.

I cross the kitchen to the fridge, bending down to peer towards the back where I've stashed the last can of Coke. I slide it out and nudge the door closed with my foot.

"Can you pour your dad and me some water please?" my mom asks as she spoons the beef onto three plates of tortillas. I go to the cabinet to get water glasses, but there aren't any full-size ones left in the cabinet.

"They're in the dishwasher," my mom says. She adds lettuce and tomatoes on top of the beef, then sprinkles the lot with shredded cheese. Ninja hovers next to her, watching and waiting for her to drop something so she can lap it up.

I pull two glasses from the dishwasher and fill them from the dispenser on the side of the fridge, then set them at the table with my Coke. "I'll empty that after dinner," I tell her.

"Thanks, sweetheart. Here you go." She passes me one of the plates piled high with tacos. Ninja follows me to the table. I sit and start shoveling food into my mouth, realizing just how hungry I am after skipping lunch.

My dad enters and takes a big sniff. "Smells delicious!" he exclaims. He heads to the sink to wash the oil and grime off his hands.

My mom joins me at the table. "So how was school today, Nell?" she asks as she gently rolls her taco into a burrito. I've tried telling her doing this doesn't make it any easier to eat, but she refuses to listen.

"'S'kay" I mumble between bites. I swallow and take a big gulp of my drink, passing bits of the meat that escaped my taco under the table to Ninja. "Actually, dad, I wanted to ask you something. We're doing a reenactment scene for Romeo and Juliet and my friends want to use your swords as props." I look at him expectantly. My mom lets out a huff in between bites of her now-falling-apart burrito.

"Well," he starts, "I'm not sure that's such a good idea, Nell. They aren't exactly toys." My mom nods in agreement.

"I know, but I kind of promised my friends it wouldn't be a problem, as long as we film here and keep them sheathed?" My voice goes up at the end, almost like a question. Which I suppose it is because, really, I don't disobey my parents, I ask for permission and do as I'm told.

Usually.

Except for that one time, which has haunted me ever since.

I hold my breath and wait for his answer. He sighs.

"Alright, you can use them, but everyone's parents have to sign off, and you need to make sure I'm home while you're filming."

"Thanks dad," I reply, smiling meekly, and my parents move on to discuss my dad's newest client. I can't help but feel as if I just forced my dad to agree to something he didn't really want to. Which in a way feels worse than if he'd just said no.

After I'm done emptying the dishwasher, I grab my backpack and head upstairs to my room, Ninja trailing behind me. I fish my beat-up iPhone out of the front zippered pocket, ignoring the texts from Shelley as I dial Brendan's house phone. His mom answers after the second ring. "Hi Mrs. Grant, it's Janelle," I say.

"Oh, hi sweetie!" she replies in her usual cheery tone. "How are you doing? How's school going?"

"Good, everything's good," I lie, gnawing on my lower lip as I scramble for something interesting to say. Thankfully, she saves me from the small talk.

"I'm glad to hear that. Let me get Brendan for you." I hear her set the phone down and shuffle away, her voice muted as she calls Brendan to the phone. I twirl a piece of thin hair that's escaped my ponytail while I wait for him to get on the line.

"Hey-oh," he finally answers with his signature greeting.

"Hi, so I talked to my dad about the swords and he said no problem," I reply. I slump down at my desk. Ninja comes over and puts her head in my lap, accepting my pets graciously. Satisfied, she slowly lowers herself to the floor, half curled around the legs of my chair. I pull my feet up underneath me and lean back.

"Nice," Brendan replies. "Send out a group text and see if everyone's around this weekend to film."

"And remind me again why *you* can't just text everyone?" I tease, already knowing it's because his mom confiscates his phone every weeknight from 5 o'clock on.

"Bite me," he laughs. "You wanna shoot for Saturday or Sunday?"

"Has to be Saturday, I've got a shift Sunday." Since school started, I've been working part-time at Reggie's Plant and Garden World in town. While I enjoy the extra cash it brings in, my favorite thing about the job is the distraction it creates. It's hard to worry about that summer night when I'm busy playing matchmaker between customers and plants.

"Saturday it is," Brendan goes on. I hear arguing in the background. "I gotta go. Meet me before first period tomorrow and we can talk more."

"Yes, your highness," I reply. Even though he can't see me, I still accompany our inside joke with my usual army salute.

After I hit *End* on my screen, I open my text messages. There are several from Shelley, asking if I'm okay after the weirdness at lunch.

All good, I lie and text back, followed by a thumbs up emoji.

I open a new message and add Shelley, Brendan, Dougie, and Tyler's contact info to it, before typing my message and hitting send:

Mercutio & Tybalt death scene, my house, Saturday @ noon, that work for everyone? Wear your most Shakespearean garments.

Duh, Tyler responds, followed by a thumbs up emoji. Brendan, of course, doesn't reply.

Who uses the word garments? Of course Dougie is the one who gives me a hard time for my language.

I'll take that as a yes, I text back. And also, shut up. I smile to myself, knowing how much Dougie hates to be told to shut up. After six minutes and twenty-one seconds of radio silence from Shelley, who usually has her phone glued to her hand and responds within seconds of getting a text, I text again.

Shell, is Saturday @ noon good?

Yes. Her one-word response tells me everything I need to know about the status of our friendship. That should make the two classes we share super comfortable and not awkward at all.

I sigh, knowing it's my fault, that Shelley's right and I just need to move on, but it seems easier said than done. With nothing left to say, I power my phone down and stick it away in my bag, choosing at least for one more day to ignore my problems in hopes they'll disappear on their own.

Friday, September 17th
Fall of Freshman Year

By the time the bell rings to end English, just about everyone has had enough of Romeo and Juliet for the day. Everyone, except for me, of course.

I slowly pack up, shoving my supplies into my backpack, cradling my worn copy of Shakespeare's tragic love story in my left hand.

"Coming?" Brendan asks, hovering near my desk.

"I'll catch up. I need to talk to Mr. Vogel about the extra credit," I tell him.

Brendan makes the symbol of a gun with his fingers, putting it to his temple. He sticks his tongue out in disgust.

"Whatever, nerd," he jokes. "See you at lunch then." He bolts for the door, along with Dougie and Tyler, eager to get to their favorite period of the day. I pretend not to notice Shelley meeting up with Bethany in the hallway, turning back to my task instead.

"Mr. Vogel?" I ask meekly as I approach my favorite teacher at the whiteboard. "Could I get another copy of the extra credit, please?"

He sets the whiteboard eraser in his hand back onto the metal tray and turns to me, a genuine smile emerging on his weathered face.

"Of course, Janelle, happy to." He shuffles around to the other side of his desk, opens a drawer, and produces a thin packet of papers, handing it over to me.

"Thanks," I tell him with a small smile before turning to go.

I fumble with my backpack, trying to gently shove the papers in as I round the corner at the end of the hall, but my attention is shattered when I walk straight into another student. His books crash to the floor, my copy of Romeo and Juliet landing on top.

"Oof!" he cries. "Sorry about that." He bends to pick up the fallen books, his black, wispy hair falling over one eye.

"No, that was totally my fault," I hurry. "I wasn't really paying attention to where I was walking." I stoop to help him pick everything up.

"Romeo and Juliet, huh?" He stands and holds out my tattered copy, and I can't help but notice how obviously cute he is. I find my gaze pulled to his soft, pink lips and the dimples that form in both cheeks as he smiles at me. "I was always more of a Hamlet fan myself," he says, drawing my attention away from his looks and back to what he's saying.

I dust off my jeans before reaching out and taking the book from him. "I like Romeo and Juliet, but Hamlet is my favorite."

"You've read it before?" His dark eyebrows go up in surprise.

"Three times, actually," I answer quietly, staring at my scuffed red Converse. I can't help but notice that he's wearing a black pair.

"Right on," he says, and smiles what seems to be another genuine smile. The warning bell rings and his smile drops. "Well, I gotta get to class, but catchya around sometime, yeah?"

Afraid of what might come out of my mouth, I give him a closed-mouth smile instead, nodding my head like I really expect to ever *'catch him around'* again. With my luck, this is probably the first and last time I'll ever actually have the chance to talk to him, and I realize as he's walking away, I didn't even get his name.

I slip into the cafeteria just as the final bell rings. I head towards my friends at our usual spot, taking great pains to avoid looking off to the other side of the room where I swear I can feel Jason's eyes on me. When I can't take it anymore, I risk a quick glance, but his back is to me, his arm wrapped protectively around Bethany's waist. His shoulders bounce as he laughs at something someone at his table said.

I hold back the urge to scream and run from the room.

When I finally make it to the safety of my lunch table, I slide into the empty seat next to Tyler. I hold in a sigh of relief when I see Shelley and Crystal are here today, huddled together, looking at something on Crystal's phone. After yesterday's lunch without them, I'm afraid to say or do anything that might jinx things and send them running back to Bethany's table.

As I settle in, I take stock of the rest of the group. Crystal's boyfriend, Petey, looks like he's asleep on the table, and Brendan and Dougie are engrossed in a heated debate about Wednesday's chess match.

"You should have castled!" Dougie yells, gesturing wildly with the fork in his left hand.

"Dude, whatever. That guy was gonna crush me no matter what I did," Brendan replies, flashing his signature crooked-tooth smirk and taking a swig from his Dr. Pepper.

"Nell, can you please settle this?" Dougie looks at me, eyebrows raised and brown eyes wide behind his black-frame glasses, like I hold all the answers.

"It's been two days, why are we still talking about this?" I question, my eyebrows pushing up in exasperation.

"She's not wrong," Brendan cackles as Dougie throws his hands up, knowing he's lost the battle.

"What took you so long?" Tyler asks as he shovels cafeteria pizza into his mouth.

"Um, I was getting the extra credit from Mr. Vogel," I reply.

"Yeah, but did you get lost between his classroom and the cafeteria?" Brendan presses, taking another sip of his drink.

"What are you, her dad?" Dougie retorts.

"Hey, inquiring minds want to know," Brendan replies, shrugging his shoulders and putting his hands up innocently.

"I, um, ran into someone in the hall," I finally say, digging through my bag not only to find my lunch card, but to distract me from saying more.

"Like, literally ran into them?" Dougie asks jokingly.

"Literally," I say.

"Like, books flying, crashing-to-the-floor type of ran into?" Dougie continues.

"Yes," I snip, giving him a firm look.

"Oh," he replies, surprised.

"Shit, hope they didn't give you a hard time," Tyler says sympathetically.

"He didn't," I say, then clamp my mouth shut, regretting the words as soon as they leave my lips.

"He?" Shelley chimes in, perking up at the prospect of a new boy, whatever was interesting on Crystal's phone forgotten.

"Yes," I squeak. "I didn't get his name. Now if you're all done grilling me," I continue before anyone can cut me off with more of the third degree, "I'd like to get my lunch." I push my chair back and scurry away before anyone can stop me.

I move through the lunch line with my tray of French fries and chicken nuggets, thinking about the mysterious Hamlet guy, as I realize I've already dubbed him. What guy willingly admits to liking Shakespeare, anyway? Out of everyone I know, I'm the only one who would ever openly admit to enjoying reading. So why didn't I open up my stupid mouth and introduce myself?

As I swipe my lunch card and walk slowly back to my table, I realize with a jolt of hopefulness that, for just one, tiny moment, my mind was no longer occupied by Jason, or Bethany, or that fateful August night. For just the briefest of moments, my mind was only consumed by the prospect of something good, something to erase the pain, the regret, the guilt of the last month.

Maybe Shelley's advice wasn't all that crazy after all.

Maybe a distraction is exactly what I need to move on.

Saturday, September 18th
Fall of Freshman Year

Before I know it, the week has come and gone, five more days of school have passed, and I'm still no closer to moving on than I was last Saturday. Or the Saturday before that. Not like I'm counting or anything.

Although my brain tells me not to, my hand has a mind of its own, slowly scrolling through my iPhone's camera roll as I rock back and forth in the chair on our back patio, stopping on every picture of Jason and me and letting myself be swept away with memories of the last year and a half together.

Before everything went wrong.

Just as I feel a small, sad smile working its way across my face, I pause when I come across a selfie of me on an unfamiliar beach, strangers lurking in the background, a bonfire blazing just off-camera, a photo I didn't even realize until just now that I had taken. I fumble with my phone, nearly dropping it on the ground as I swipe to delete the picture, desperate to remove any evidence of that summer night, wishing that with the same swipe of my finger, I could erase the memory from my mind.

As I feel my heart begin to race and my throat go dry, an incoming text *dings*, creating a welcome distraction from the rabbit hole I was inches from falling down.

Be there in ten, Dougie's text reads.

I refocus my thoughts and energy on the day ahead of me, slipping my phone into my jeans and making my way into the house.

Just stay focused on right now, don't think about him, don't think about that night, I remind myself as I begin to gather supplies for our video shoot.

I pour a five-pound bag of ice into a red cooler my mom left out on the counter, shaking it slightly to get the ice to settle in between the eight bottles of water and five cans of Coke I've filled it with. I close the lid and set three bags of chips on top, then I heft the cooler and snacks back outside to the patio. I set everything down next to our glass-topped picnic table and settle back into one of the rockers along the edge of the deck.

I lean back in my chair and close my eyes, trying to focus on the task ahead of me today instead of the horror behind me. I pretend I'm transported back in time, to Shakespearean London, as a young thespian preparing for his debut performance. My mind takes me even further, to fair Verona, imagining for a moment that I *am* Mercutio, that I embody what it takes to be a strong, right-hand man to Romeo, that I have what it takes to push the envelope, even with death beckoning. That I refuse to back down, even if it means perishing.

If only I could embody Mercutio's bold fearlessness in my real life.

"Earth to Nell?" My eyes flutter open at the sound of Dougie's voice. He and Brendan are standing in front of me, peering down. Dougie's face is all scrunched up, his mouth slightly agape, waving his hand in front of my face. Brendan's head is cocked, his lips curled up in a slight smile.

"Sorry," I mutter, "just trying to get into character."

"Well, it'd be a lot easier if you were in costume already," Brendan says as he plops down into the chair to the left of me.

"Yeah, what happened to *'bring your best Shakespearean garments'*?" Dougie teases, leaning against the railing.

"Any sign of Shelley and Tyler?" I ask, ignoring their teasing comments, lacking the energy to volley one back at them.

"Should be here any minute," Dougie replies.

Brendan grabs a bag of Fritos off the table, poised to tear into it.

"Hey! Those are for *after* we shoot the scene," I say, snatching the bag out of his grip before he can open it.

"What? I'm hungry, and you promised there'd be snacks," he pouts, trying to get me to cave.

"After," I scold him, and put the chips on the table out of his reach. I hear the crunch of gravel. "Sounds like they're here. Why don't you all head down to the paddock and I'll meet you there? I have to grab the costumes and swords."

"I can help you," Brendan offers but I wave him away.

They head towards the other end of my backyard where the horse paddock is. Luckily, the horses are tucked away in their stalls so we can use the open space to set up our scene. I watch them go, then turn and head inside. I go down into the basement where we have all our Halloween costumes and leftovers from previous school plays stored. I grab the pile I set aside earlier, every article of clothing that could pass as Shakespearean. On my way back outside, I poke my head into the garage where my dad is tinkering with his tools.

"We're ready," I tell him. Ninja perks up at the sound of my voice. "Stay, girl," I say, and she lays her head back down.

"Be right there, sweetheart," my dad answers. I wander back through the house and out to the back yard. As I get closer to where my friends are waiting for me, I hear bickering. I round the corner of the barn and of course, it's Shelley and Brendan arguing.

"Well at least I thought to bring *something*," Brendan is telling her.

Shelley has her hand on her hip, in her typical Shelley way. She looks over at me as I approach. "Brendan thought it would make sense to bring a fire poker to use as a prop in a Shakespeare play."

He holds it out by way of explanation.

"I mean, it's better than nothing?" I say tentatively. "Plus I only have four swords, and there's five of us. What do you guys think?" I turn towards the rest of the group.

Tyler shrugs his shoulders. "Whatever you think."

"Not helping." I give him a look and turn to Dougie. "Thoughts?" I ask him.

"It's rustic and sharp, and they were readily available during the time..." Dougie starts, cupping his chin in thought.

"Get to the point, bro," Brendan chimes in.

Dougie glares at him. "I think it works."

I look back at Shelley and shrug. "Sorry, majority wins."

She crosses her arms and mumbles a dejected *'whatever.'* "Can we just get this over with?" she asks. With impeccable timing, my dad appears, medieval swords in hand and Ninja in tow.

"Alright, Nell, remember what we discussed, keep them sheathed, no blades out."

I give him a small nod, and he turns to my friends. "All of your parents are aware you'll be using these, and are okay with it, right?" He's met with a *'yessir'* and a *'yes Mr. Beckley'* and many nodding heads. "Good. If any of you end up in the hospital over this, you'll never be invited back, got it?" More head nods and looks of sheer terror from my friends; they know my dad doesn't mess around.

He hands them off to me. "Thanks again, dad." I give him a tiny smile. He waves and turns back toward the house, calling Ninja after him.

"Ready?" I turn back towards my friends.

"Let the show begin!" Brendan booms, and Dougie slaps the clapperboard to signal Tyler, who starts recording.

Fifty-eight minutes and thirty-six seconds later, Brendan yells "*cut*!" to end our final take. Though Dougie and I are laying on the ground in apparent death, we all managed to make it through the scene without any actual injuries. At least, not any physical ones.

"So is that it, then?" Shelley demands, hand on her hip again.

"Yeah, I think we got it all," Tyler replies, flicking through the shots on his iPad.

"Alright, great," she continues, "You ready to get me home?"

"Sure thing," he answers. He sticks his hand in his pocket and retrieves his keys.

"Cool, well, let us know if you guys like, need help editing or whatever." Shelley picks a piece of imaginary lint off of her once-white button-up, collared shirt.

"Will do," Brendan replies curtly.

"Cool. See you Monday then." She turns and stomps off, Tyler trailing in her wake of dust.

"See ya, guys," he says sheepishly as he shuffles away.

"God, why does she always have to be like that!" Brendan practically shouts once she's out of earshot.

"I mean, she's always been kind of a bitch," Dougie chimes in. "That isn't new."

"Just seems like it's gotten worse since we started high school," Brendan replies.

I almost come to Shelley's defense, knowing that Brendan is wrong, that her attitude didn't shift just because we started high school. The shift happened when I stopped confiding in her, when I refused to tell her the truth about why Jason and I broke up.

It's my fault Shelley's become so cold.

"Guys, c'mon, she's one of my best friends," I say instead, hoping it's enough to put an end to the debate.

"I dunno, she just seems kinda bossy, Nell. She's always telling you what she thinks with that big, fat mouth of hers," Brendan goes on. "And she's always trying to get you to do what *she* wants. It's annoying."

"Yeah," Dougie agrees.

"Well right now *you're* being annoying," I snap. "Come on, let's just clean all this up and go take a break. You can eat all the Fritos you want, now," I remind Brendan, knowing if he moves on, Dougie will follow suit.

Luckily, it works. Brendan blows out a long sigh, then hoists a sword in one hand and his fire poker in the other, trudging off towards the house.

Dougie, clapperboard still in hand, grabs the remaining three swords and I gather the various clothes strewn about the ground. I take one last look around to make sure we got it all before turning to shuffle back up to the deck behind my friends, the very ones who would follow me into battle, even to the death, if I needed them to, just like Mercutio did for Romeo.

I just hope it doesn't actually come to that.

*****

Later that night, as I'm on my laptop reviewing the day's takes from the file Tyler sent me, my phone chirps with a notification from Instagram. I lean back in my desk chair and swipe my phone from the nightstand, punching in my four-digit passcode and pulling up the photo-sharing app on my screen.

The notification alerts me that I've been tagged in three new photos, and I swipe to see what they are. Brendan has posted a bunch of candid shots from today's filming, photos I hadn't even realized he'd snapped at the time. There's a selfie of himself, holding all of the swords. He must have taken it when I was changing into my outfit, because I don't remember him posing like that. He's captioned it **swords never get tired**, one of his favorite quotes from Kill Bill Volume I. I double-tap to like the photo, then think of a clever reply, using a line from Troy that I hope he'll appreciate.

You have your swords. I have my tricks. We play with the toys the gods give us.

I hit *enter* and swipe for the next picture, which turns out to be a photo of Dougie and me locked in our fight scene, Dougie as Tybalt moments away from killing me as Mercutio. And then of course, there's a photo of me actually dying on the ground as Dougie runs off in the distance. The final tag is a shot of me and Tyler as we practiced wielding our swords before the camera was rolling. Among the photos of me are other candids of Dougie and Tyler, as well as a few more selfies of Brendan. Unsurprisingly, there are no photos of Shelley, save for the fight scene that everyone's in, where she lingers in the background.

I "like" them all, then swipe back to my newsfeed to see what everyone else I follow has been up to, refusing to fully admit that more than anything, I want to see what Jason's been up to.

I scroll past some nature shots that my aunt has shared from her backyard in Portland, and a boomerang of Emma Roberts getting a cake smashed in her face before I finally come up on Jason's latest post.

I feel the blood drain from my face as I stare at his smiling face, arm draped around Bethany's shoulder as they cram into the frame with a bunch of others I mostly recognize from the skate park. But it isn't until I realize where they're standing that my stomach drops.

That picnic table. That towering willow tree. That sparkling lake in the background.

I utter a small cry when I realize that he's at Lake Wallenpaupack, *our lake*, with *her*.

Only it isn't our lake anymore, I remind myself. I made sure of that forty-two days, sixteen hours and eleven seconds ago.

It's their lake now.

And I have no one to blame but myself.

Sunday, September 19th
Fall of Freshman Year

At work the next day, I'm crouched down, digging through a cardboard box as I search for printer paper, when I hear a familiar voice above me.

"Excuse me, could you help me?"

As I scramble out from under the check-out counter of Reggie's Plant and Garden World, I knock my head against the underside of the counter, nearly dropping the roll of printer paper clutched in my grasp.

"Fff...ahhh..." I catch myself before I can finish the word. Rubbing the side of my head, I emerge from below the counter and straighten up, coming face to face with Hamlet guy.

He cocks his head to the side and smiles. "Hey. You okay?" he adds.

"Um, hi," I squeak back, fumbling with the roll of printer paper in my hand. "Yeah, you just caught me off guard is all. Uh, what can I help with you?" I set the roll on the counter and wipe my sweating hands on the leg of my jeans, trying to calm my thumping heart.

"I'm looking for a gift," he says.

"For your girlfriend?" I blurt out. I clamp my mouth shut, afraid of what might come out of it next. Luckily, he just chuckles at my stupidity.

"No, no girlfriend," he replies, staring at me intently with his dark brown eyes. I swallow hard.

"It's for my mom, actually," he continues. "Her birthday is coming up, and she loves to garden, so I thought maybe I could get her some new plants. But honestly, I know nothing about plants." He chuckles again and shrugs.

"Well, you came to the right place!" I practically shout back. Just when I'm ready to pass him off to a different salesperson, or really *anyone* else who can save me from my own uncontrollable mouth, the phone rings. "Just a sec," I say, holding up a finger to him.

"No worries, I'll just be over here waiting for you." He gives me another smile and turns toward the back corner of the shop where we have a stand of greeting cards and small plant tchotchkes.

I pick up the portable receiver. “Thanks for calling Reggie’s Plant and Garden World, this is Janelle, how can I help you?” I rattle off our standard greeting, eyeing him as he rifles through the cards, reading them and smiling to himself.

The caller on the other end, a regular named Mrs. Williams, wants to reschedule her delivery of mulch for next weekend. I grab the delivery schedule off the wall behind me, flip to the new date and pencil her in.

“And when was your original delivery scheduled for?” I ask, flipping a few more pages and watching as he picks up a small garden gnome statue, turning it over to look for the price tag.

“Okay, you’re all set, Mrs. Williams, we’ll see you at 11 am on the 29th.” I hang up with her and stick the phone in the pocket of my green apron. I take a deep breath and walk towards him.

You can do this, Janelle, I tell myself. *You need to do this, to move on.*

After all, Jason has.

He turns toward me as I approach, holding up a pair of Garden Genie gloves with attached claws. “I didn’t realize this is where Wolverine shops,” he says with a serious face.

I suppress a sarcastic reply to his lame joke. “They just make it easier to dig in the dirt,” I tell him.

"Ah, so I guess I'll be needing a pair in order to dig my own grave after that terrible joke then, huh?" he says as he sets the gloves back on the shelf.

"It was pretty bad," I say, shuffling my feet. "So, you're looking for a birthday gift for your mom, right?" I ask, trying to steer us back to familiar territory.

"Yeah, I thought maybe getting her some plants would be a good idea, but now I'm second guessing it. I have no idea what kind to get her." His face falls in disappointment.

"Well, can you tell me what her garden's like?" I ask, walking him towards the door to the greenhouse.

"Big. Full of plants," he shrugs.

"I mean can you tell me where in the yard it is? What kind of sunlight it gets? Does it get steady water when it rains? That sort of thing."

"Ooooh! Yeah, that makes more sense." He taps his palm to his forward in a *'duh'* gesture. "Um, she has some flowers planted along the front of the house, but the majority of everything is in the backyard. It's pretty open, no trees or anything in the way, so I guess it would get sun and rain all the time."

I turn down a few different aisles, listening as he tells me more about his mom's preferences and gardening experience. We settle on a few hydrangea bushes and daffodil bulbs, which will bloom nicely in the spring. I grab a garden wagon and load everything up, then wheel it back into the main building to ring him up.

"How do you know about all this stuff?" he asks as he trails beside me. "I feel like I wouldn't be able to tell the difference between one plant and the next." He scratches at his head, then smooths down the tuft of black hair that sticks up out of place.

"I didn't know any of it at first. But I've picked up most of it since I started. There's still a few things I'm not so sure about. It takes time to learn it all," I tell him as we approach the check-out desk.

"You must really like plants, then, huh?" He asks, leaning against the counter and propping his chin in his hand.

"Actually, I like nature, but I hate gardening. I don't like dirt. It gets under your fingernails and takes forever to scrub out." I smile sheepishly up at him, embarrassed by my germophobic tendencies.

He straightens up and laughs a deep, genuine laugh. "A girl who hates dirt working in a plant store. Gotta love the irony."

"Yep, the irony is definitely not lost on me," I smirk. "Normally you have to be at least sixteen to work here but my mom's best friend is the manager and she pulled some strings, so it would have been kinda hard to turn it down," I explain to him. "I'm just grateful for the job and the extra cash it provides." *And more importantly, the distraction it gives me,* I almost add.

I ring up his plants and give him the total. "Wait," he says, and scurries back over to the stand of greeting cards. He turns the rotating stand, scanning the cards until he lands on the one he's looking for. He snatches it and lays it on the counter. "Can't forget the birthday card."

"That's nice of you," I say as I add the card to his bill. "I actually don't like birthday cards, myself, so I never buy them for other people, even though it always makes me feel a tad guilty."

Why am I telling him all of this? Shut up, Janelle.

He hands me his debit card and I glance down at his name. *Keith Felding*, I mumble, not realizing I've said it aloud.

"Nice to officially meet you," he says, and I look up from the register to meet his gaze. "Janelle, right?"

"How did you…" I start.

"You said it before, when you answered the phone," he informs me.

"Right," I stutter, shocked he was paying attention to that. I swipe the card and hand it back to him, sliding the keypad across the counter for him to enter his pin. I look away while he punches four digits into the machine.

"So, now that it's official and we know each other's names," he begins, as he slides his card back into his brown leather wallet, "would you maybe want to hang out sometime? Y'know, outside the confines of a greenhouse?"

The receipt printer makes an angry, garbled noise, telling me it's out of paper, making me jump.

"Sure.." I trail off, unsure if he's serious. I grab the roll of printer paper I set down on the counter earlier, flip open the machine, and feed it through. The noise stops and his receipt pops up.

"I mean, only if you want to," he interjects.

"No, that's not...I mean, yes, of course I want to..." I hand him his receipt and clear my throat, hoping the heat I feel rising to my cheeks isn't noticeable. "Yes, I'd like that," I try again.

He chuckles. "Okay, cool. Why don't you give me your number?" he says, unlocking his cell phone and passing it to me.

I look down at it, a moment of deja vu causing me to hesitate. My breath catches in my throat and I swallow, trying to clear away the nausea that's building inside of me.

This isn't like last time, I remind myself, fighting the wave of nervousness threatening to crash over me.

After what feels like minutes, but is really only seconds, I feel my hands reach out to take the phone, fingers trembling ever so slightly as I punch in my number. I hold it back out to him, hoping he doesn't notice my hands shaking as I pass it off.

He hits *Dial* and I feel my back pocket vibrate. He ends the call and slips his phone in the front pocket of his jeans.

"Cool, so now I'll definitely catchya 'round." He smiles his perfectly straight white teeth at me, giving me another one of those intense stares. I swallow again and find my voice.

"Fersure," I blurt, mashing my words together.

"Thanks again for your help today. I'll text you later," he says, and starts to turn away.

"Yeah, definitely," is all I can say.

"Wait, one more thing." He stops and turns back around to face me head-on. I brace myself, waiting for any sort of inkling that this will turn out exactly like it did the last time I was in this situation, that I was right in thinking it could only ever be one way for me with boys, but he simply continues talking.

"You said you don't like birthday cards, but I find that hard to believe. Who doesn't like getting a card for their birthday?" He tilts his head to the side, waiting for my answer.

"It's not that I don't like getting them," I start, unsure where he's going with this. "I just don't see the point of them. You pick out a pre-written card for someone and give it to them, but it has no real meaning, because you didn't even bother to write it yourself. If it's handmade, that's one thing. But most people don't take the time to make a handmade card for anyone, so why bother with a mass-produced version? The pre-written ones usually end up in the trash anyway, so why create extra waste? I dunno, I just don't see the purpose."

As I finish rambling, I clamp my mouth shut tight, sure I've blown it. He's staring at me the way a scientist stares intently at a microbe through a lens, as if he's unsure what this delicate and unfamiliar organism before him is. It's unnerving, because only one other person has ever stared at me like that. My throat starts to go dry as I second guess my decision to give him my number, and I wonder if this is really such a good idea after all, Shelley be damned. Before I can give it any more thought, he interrupts my brain with a response.

"I'll have to keep that in mind," he smiles slyly. "See you soon, Janelle," he says, and walks out the door.

I watch as he climbs into his car and backs out of the parking lot, waiting until he's pulled out onto the main road before I collapse against the counter, my heart beating wildly beneath my chest.

If Shelley were here, I know she'd be proud of me for putting myself out there and trying to move on. I breathe in deeply through my nose, trying to calm down, reminding myself that I'm single now, and giving a boy my number is perfectly normal at this point.

This time, instead of letting the unknown number linger like a secret I know I shouldn't keep, I immediately save it to my contacts.

Telling myself it won't be like last time.

That it *can't* be like last time.

Sunday, August 5th
Summer Before Freshman Year

About an hour and a half after getting to the beach, Janelle rolled over onto her back and smoothed the beach towel on the sand beneath her. She glanced over at her sister in the beach chair next to her, smiling at something on her phone.

Probably another text from Brett, Janelle thought. *God forbid she puts the phone down and actually has a conversation with me.*

Frustrated, she sat up and grabbed a bottle of sunblock from her straw beach bag. She shook it back and forth to mix it, ignoring her sister's incessant reminders that it wasn't necessary to do so. She squirted a good-sized blob into her hands and rubbed them together, smearing them down her arms, legs, and across her bare stomach. She squirted a dime-sized bit into her hands once more and rubbed it into her face, scrunching her eyes closed to avoid getting any in them.

"You missed a spot," Lauren barked. Janelle's eyes popped open.

"Where?" she asked.

"Right here," she said, scratching at the left side of her nose to indicate the spot. Janelle rubbed at the right side of her own nose. Lauren sighed. "Other left," she instructed. Growling, Janelle swiped at the other side of her nose until she couldn't feel any more lotion there.

"Did I get it all?" she asked her sister.

"Yeah," Lauren shrugged, eyes back on her phone.

"Ugh," Janelle mumbled, and flopped back down on the towel. She tossed the sunblock back in her bag and grabbed her own phone.

If Lauren's going to ignore me, I can ignore her right back.

She opened Instagram and scrolled through her feed, stopping to "like" a photo of Brendan and Dougie holding up life-size chess pieces like lightsabers, an action shot of Jason doing a trick on one of the bike ramps at the skatepark, and a zoomed-in photo of a baby bird that her aunt had taken.

She kept scrolling until she came across a photo of Shelley, Crystal, Bethany, Jason, and a couple other guys whose names she could never remember crowded on top of a picnic table near a familiar-looking lake. The girls were squished in the middle of the table, Shelley dead center, of course, flashing her brightest smile, with Crystal and Bethany flanking her. One of the boys had his arm around Crystal's shoulder- *were they a thing, now?-* and Janelle couldn't help but notice how tightly squeezed together Jason and Bethany were, Bethany's hand lightly grazing Jason's leg.

I'm just being paranoid, right? C'mon, Janelle, don't be ridiculous, she thought.

Her finger hovered over the "like" button a minute before she finally pressed it. She noted the timestamp, then closed out of Instagram and pulled up her texts.

Did you go to the lake yesterday? she texted Jason, referring to the biggest lake in their area, Lake Wallenpaupack.

Yeah, the guys wanted 2 go. Shelley n them tagged along 2, u no how they are. I no we were supposed 2 go when u got bak, but it's not a big deal, we can go again, he replied.

Except it *was* a big deal. It was supposed to be *their* lake, where they had their first date. Janelle had asked Jason if they could go at the end of summer as their last summer adventure together, just the two of them, before school resumed. She was nervous of the way things were about to change once they all left middle school behind and started high school, and she wanted this one last feeling of familiarity to cling to. Jason had assured her that not much would change, they were all going to stay friends and the two of them would still be a thing; the only difference might be everyone's physical changes that happen around that age.

But he was wrong; things *had* already changed. He'd promised Janelle this one thing, something that really meant a lot to her, even if he couldn't understand why, and he'd broken that promise with as much nonchalance as if she'd asked him for the time. If he didn't care about her feelings, or how important this was to her, what else would he disregard?

After spending the rest of the morning staring out at the water in thought while her sister alternated between texting Brett and napping on the sand, Janelle had finally had enough.

"I'm going shopping," she announced, standing up from her beach chair.

Her sister looked up, noticing the grimace on Janelle's face. "A little retail therapy could do you some good," she said, and went back to her phone.

"Yeah, exactly," Janelle mumbled, and stormed off the beach.

She crossed the street back towards their beach house, noticing the car wasn't in the driveway, her parents still out for the day, then hung a left down the sidewalk towards the main drag. She shuffled along the pavement slowly, stopping to peer into windows and people-watch as families on their own holidays shopped and dined at the cluster of stores up and down the promenade.

After walking the main street for a few minutes, Janelle turned down a side street and came up on a surf shop she'd never been in before. She scooted through the door as it closed behind a woman who was leaving.

Though her fingers worked the racks, absentmindedly browsing the array of clothing for sale, she couldn't get her mind to stop thinking about that picture, and Jason's oblivious text.

"That would look really good on you."

Janelle jumped, startled by the unexpected voice, and turned to see where it had come from, the purple tank top she was admiring still clutched in her hands. She blushed as she came face to face with a tall, blue-eyed boy, his blonde hair sticking out messily from under a black Volcom hat.

"Thanks," she replied quietly. "Shopping usually helps calm me down when I'm upset, but I just can't seem to pick out anything good today." She stuck the shirt back on the rack and shrugged.

"Can't imagine what a pretty girl like you could be so worried about," he continued, leaning his elbow on a nearby rack.

Janelle laughed. "I'm about to start high school, there's plenty to worry about."

"High school, okay," he nodded, "so you're what, like fourteen? Fifteen?" He eyed her up and down, trying to gauge her age.

"Just turned fourteen last month. You?"

"I'm coming up on the big one-eight in a few weeks." He held up four fingers to Janelle. "Not that big of a difference, huh?" He cocked his head and smiled. He squinted his eyes at her, trying to place her. "I've never seen you around before, so I'm guessing you're a tourist, not a townie?"

"Yeah. Is it that obvious?" she laughed.

"Yours is a face I'd definitely remember seeing around town."

Janelle met his gaze, locking eyes with him. She could feel herself blush again, the heat creeping its way up her neck into her cheeks.

"So how long you here for?" he went on, seemingly unfazed by her embarrassment.

"Just a week. We actually come here every summer, but I've never been in this store before. I guess I usually stick to the tourist spots." Janelle shrugged again, trying to feign nonchalance. She wasn't sure it was working. She could feel her fingers curling under, the nails inching closer to her palms and she told herself to relax, flexing her fingers back out and hoping he didn't notice.

An older guy in board shorts and flip flops approached them. "Travis, we just got this week's shipment in, can you take care of it?"

The boy named Travis turned toward him and flashed a set of perfectly straight, white teeth. "You got it, boss." The older guy sauntered off and Travis turned back to Janelle. "Duty calls. But we should hang out while you're in town. I can show you around, introduce you to some of the local spots the tourists don't know about." He slipped his hands into his pockets. "Do you surf?"

"No, but I've always wanted to learn. I say I'm going to every summer, but then I never get around to it."

He nodded. "Okay, we're definitely going surfing."

He pulled his phone out of his pocket and swiped the screen, tapping in his passcode before handing it to Janelle. "Here, give me your number and I'll text you mine."

Janelle looked down at the phone, hesitant. After a beat, she swallowed her unease, took the phone, and punched in her name and number before handing it back.

It was just surf lessons.

Travis looked down at her info. "Nice to meet you, Janelle," he said, looking back up and meeting her gaze. He typed something into his phone before slipping it back into his shorts. Janelle felt her back pocket buzz with an incoming text.

"Check and make sure you got it," Travis told her. She pulled her phone out, a message from an unknown number that said hey, it's Travis.

She held the phone up to him and smiled weakly. "Got it."

"Cool," he nodded. "I gotta get back to work, but I'll text you later. Weather's gonna be dope tomorrow, so I'll text you the details and we'll get out on the water." He backed away from Janelle, his eyes still locked on hers. "See ya then."

"Yeah, see ya then," she mimicked uncomfortably.

He turned and disappeared into the back room. As Janelle watched him go, she felt another buzz from her phone, still clutched in her hand. She looked at the screen, a new message from Jason popping up below Travis's, reminding her she still hadn't answered his last text from this morning.

Don't b mad xoxo, it read.

Janelle glanced from her phone back to the door Travis had gone through, a knot tightening in her stomach.

She cleared both texts from her home screen and slipped her phone back into her pocket. If Jason could have fun without her, she could do the same.

After all, it was just surf lessons.

Right?

Monday, September 20th
Fall of Freshman Year

I'm tapping my pencil against my Geometry notebook in Monday morning study hall, pretending to study, when I hear Shelley and Crystal at the door. I look up as they come barreling into the room, their arms linked, giggling like they just shared an intimate joke. I stiffen as they approach, an unshakeable sinking feeling taking hold of me. With the way Shelley left things after Saturday's filming, I can't help but feel there's something they're keeping from me.

"Hiii," I squeal, overly enthusiastic as they arrive.

"Hey," they both reply simultaneously, settling into the seats on either side of me. Crystal pulls her Biology textbook from her green messenger bag and flips to chapter three. Shelley has her planner in hand and looks over at me.

"Don't worry, *mom,*" she says, "I already did all my homework this weekend." I can hear the judgment in her voice. I clench my fists in my lap, digging my nails into my palms, where they create small, crescent dents in the skin. My fingers itch for a paperclip or safety pin, and the privacy of a bathroom stall. I inhale sharply through my nose and release my fists.

"So how was everyone's weekend?" I move on, trying to sound breezy and nonchalant, but it comes out squeaky and uncomfortable instead.

"It was good," Crystal starts, giving Shelley a look.

"What?" I ask, watching Shelley's face for any clues.

"Well, we went to the skatepark yesterday with Petey and everyone," Crystal continues. By "everyone" I know she means Bethany and Jason, too.

"That's cool," I say, trying to keep my voice from cracking. I go back to my notebook, doodling swirls down the margins, too distracted to actually attempt the extra credit math problems I requested last week.

"Yeah," Shelley replies. "After awhile it got boring though. How many hours can you just sit there and watch the guys going back and forth on the ramps?" She flicks her hair off her shoulders in her typical Shelley fashion. "So I texted my friend, Maggie, from band. She plays the flute, too. Apparently there was some shindig going on at this junior guy's house. Steve something or other. So we headed over there for a bit. It was pretty chill." She cracks her knuckles like it's no big deal that they ended up at some random upperclassman's party on a Sunday afternoon.

"We would have texted you, but we knew you were working," Crystal adds, biting her lip.

"No worries, I get it," I reply. Although I can't help but feel like they wouldn't have invited me even if I *hadn't* been working.

"So what about you?" Crystal asks, polite as ever as she skims her textbook. "How was work?"

I look over at Shelley, who is absorbed in her planner.

"It was okay," I shrug. "Just another day at work."

I gnaw at the inside of my cheek, wanting to say more, wanting to tell them about Keith, and how I'm finally taking Shelley's advice, as hard as it may be. But as I sit there contemplating the right words, Shelley pulls out her phone, smiling to herself as she furiously texts something to someone that isn't me, and I feel the tiny bit of courage I almost mustered fade away. Brendan's words from Saturday whisper in my head. It was true I had felt Shelley pulling away recently, but had she really changed that much since the summer, since high school started?

Or was it just me that had changed?

*****

As the rest of the morning passes, I feel guilty for not telling my friends about Keith. Desperate to avoid any more secrets than I already have, desperate to go back to a time when we told each other everything, I decide during English class that I'll fill them in at lunch. Because what's the point of having girlfriends if you can't share these moments with them, anyway?

As I space out through Mr. Vogel's lecture on the expectations of marriage during the Renaissance era, I wonder how I should start the conversation. Do I start from our original chance encounter in the hallway and work my way forward? Or do I tell them about how he walked into my place of employment yesterday and then work backwards through the rest of it? Knowing Shelley, she'll want every minute detail, regardless of how unimportant it may seem.

I'm contemplating the pros and cons of either scenario when my thoughts are interrupted by a tiny vibration against my leg. When Mr. Vogel's back is turned, I slip my phone out of my pocket to find a mass group thread from Will, our chess team captain.

Practice moved to 2nd floor lab, same time, it says. I look over at Dougie and Brendan, who are reading the same messages on their phones. They both look over and give me a nod. I reply to Will with a thumbs up emoji. I'm about to put my phone away when it vibrates in my hand again. Assuming it's just another reply in the group thread, I give it a quick glance, intending to put it away without opening it. But the name *Keith Felding* stops me in my tracks. I draw in a quick breath through my teeth and swipe open the text, cradling my phone in my lap to hide it from view.

So I know we only just met, but I kinda can't stop thinking about you.

My heart skips a beat, although I can't tell if it's from excitement or fear. I have no clue how to respond to that, but luckily I see the three dots appear to show he's still typing, so I wait to see what he'll say next before I answer.

That probably makes me clingy or something, I know, but you seem really cool, so I just wanted to tell you. He follows it with a smiley emoji.

Unsure how to reply, I simply text back my own smiley emoji. I glance up at Mr. Vogel, who's writing something on the board vigorously. I snatch my pen off my desk, jotting down the notes into my notebook, wondering if the smiley emoji sends the wrong message.

Wondering what message I even want to send him in the first place.

I feel my phone buzz again as another text comes through.

Any chance of a quick meet-up between classes? Say, that same spot in A hallway where I mowed you down that one time? He follows this one with a wink face emoji. Moisture begins to form under my arms at the thought of seeing him again.

It's different. He's different. You're different, I think, trying to convince myself. After another forty-two seconds of silence, I finally reply.

Sure.

Told ya I'd see you soon, he replies. I look at the clock. Eleven minutes and nineteen seconds to go. I furiously scribble the notes I missed, trying to muster up the carefree confidence I once had when it came to boys.

As class wraps up, I try not to wonder if I'm about to walk into the exact same situation that put me in this whole mess to begin with.

At the bell for lunch, I'm beginning to second-guess the agreement to meet Keith in the hallway. Out of time to back out of it, I tell myself to just go and get it over with.

It can't be <u>*that*</u> *bad, can it?* I remind myself as I hustle out the door before my friends can stop me. *This is the same guy who made a dad joke at the plant shop, not some show-off surfer boy trying to charm you into falling for his tricks.*

I blow past Bethany lingering in the hallway, who gives me a startled look. I assume that means Shelley and Crystal aren't sitting with me at lunch today, but I'm too nervous about Keith to care. I hear Brendan call my name but I just keep going. I try to slow myself from deliberately running, but my feet have a mind of their own. Of course, my eagerness lands me at that special corner of the hallway with extra time to spare; Keith is nowhere to be seen.

"What the hell?" Brendan says, slightly out of breath as he, Dougie, and Tyler wheel up next to me.

"What?" I ask, pretending I don't know exactly what he means. I stretch my neck to see down the end of the hall past the throng of students leaving their classrooms.

"Way to wait up," he goes on.

"Sorry," I answer, sheepishly.

"Hey." I hear Keith's voice, one that's becoming familiar, behind me. My pulse races as I turn and meet his gaze.

"Hey yourself." I force down the desire to take a step backwards and instead plaster a giant closed-mouth smile on my face.

My friends, while smart in every class in school, seem oblivious as they continue to hover nearby. I turn slightly back towards them. "See you guys at lunch." I give them all death stares. Tyler gives a quick wave and scurries off, and Dougie raises his eyebrows questioningly before following. Brendan locks eyes with Keith and stares him down before slowly turning and sauntering off.

"Friends of yours?" Keith asks.

"Yeah, sorry about them," I breathe. "They can act a bit like brothers, y'know, overprotective and all that." I wring my hands, silently cursing Brendan for ruining the chance at whatever this even is, but Keith just chuckles.

"No biggie. It's good to have friends like that," he replies. "So, I was hoping we could hang out soon?" he goes on. "Like, maybe after school today?"

"Oh," I say, my face falling.

"Only if you want to," he adds, unsure.

"No, I definitely do," I reply, unsure if I actually mean it. "It's just, I have chess practice after school today." I click the toes of my scuffed red Converse together, waiting for him to retract his invitation once he learns what a nerd I am. Well, what an even *bigger* nerd, considering he already knows I like Shakespeare so much.

"Oh," he says, and I wait for the awkwardness as he tries to figure out a way to politely pretend he never met me. But he just smiles. "Cool."

"Really?" I blurt like an idiot, and cover my mouth with my hand. As if I can stuff the words back in.

He laughs, nodding. "First Shakespeare and now chess? I'm impressed," he goes on. "Although I will admit I'm also slightly intimidated. I've never dated a girl so much smarter than me."

I gulp hard at the word *dated* and try not to break out in hives. The warning bell saves me from the embarrassing reply that was inevitably about to escape my mouth. He looks up at the sound.

"So how 'bout tomorrow after school then? We could take a drive down to the Swirly Cone for some ice cream before it closes for the season?" he asks.

"Um, sure," I answer.

"Cool, meet me in the student lot after school tomorrow," he says.

"Okay."

"Well," he continues, "parting is such sweet sorrow…" he trails off, waiting for me to continue the quote. I can't tell if he's trying to bait me, or if he's just as much of a Shakespeare geek as me. I pray it's the latter, and let myself be swept away, even if just for a minute.

"That I shall say good night till it be 'morrow," I finish.

He smiles. "Text me after your practice, 'kay?" He starts walking backwards away from me, locking eyes with me as he goes.

"'Kay," is all I can say. He gives me a sly smile before finally turning away and walking off. I feel cemented to the floor, and I have to remind my feet to move as the final bell rings, making me officially late to my first class period ever.

I fumble with the cafeteria doors, finally making my way in and reminding myself to keep my eyes trained on my table, straight ahead, so as to avoid seeing any unwanted PDA between Jason and Bethany. As I approach my lunch table, I try to wipe the shell-shocked look off my face before my friends see it and give me a hard time.

Too late.

"Who was that?" Brendan interrupts Dougie mid-sentence as he clambers on about some old school M. Night Shyamalan movie.

"This guy I met the other day," I reply, settling into the empty chair next to Tyler.

"Met where? Does he have a name?" Brendan interrogates.

"What's with the third degree, dude?" Dougie asks, shoving a handful of fries into his mouth.

"Nothing," Brendan leans back in his chair and crosses his arms, eyeing me. "Just want to be sure Nell isn't getting caught up with a rando."

"I'll be fine, thank you," I tell him, unsure if the words will ever actually be true. "And he's not a rando," I continue. "His name is Keith. He's the one who bumped into me in the hallway last week. He came into Reggie's yesterday and asked me out." I twist the truth a bit on that last detail, because he didn't come into the shop *to* ask me out, he did so *after* realizing I worked there. But, considering Keith just referred to me as someone he would date only moments ago, it doesn't feel so dishonest to say it this way. Although I'm still not entirely sure how I feel about the idea of dating someone new. Someone older.

Someone like *him*.

I shake away the thought, fish my lunch card out of my wallet, and stand up. "Now if you'll excuse me," I say, and walk away from the table before anyone can say anything else.

As I walk through the cafeteria, I let myself glance over at the table where Shelley, Crystal, and Petey are sitting with Bethany, Jason, and the rest of his friends. They don't notice me watching them, no one looks up to meet my gaze, and I realize with a pang that I wish they would. After practicing in my head how I wanted to tell Shelley and Crystal all about Keith, I'm left disappointed knowing I won't be able to, at least not for the time being. Though the guys seemed interested enough to hear about him, telling your guy friends about a new love interest isn't quite the same as telling your girl friends.

I sigh, grab a lunch tray, and get in the lunch line behind a tall girl in a basketball uniform. I wonder if things between my friends and me will ever get back to normal, or if this shared custody with Bethany and Jason *is* my new normal.

I know it's my fault things changed, I just hope it's not too late to change them back.

Monday, September 20th
Fall of Freshman Year

"Janelle!" Will calls my name again and I snap back to reality, blinking away the memory of the first time I finally got Jason to play chess with me.

Pretending I don't see his face in every opponent that sits across the chess board from me.

"What?" I ask, confused. Will is staring at me as if he's plotting my murder. I understand now how he managed to secure his spot as our team captain.

"Are you gonna make a move? You've been staring at the board for like, ten minutes now," he says. I risk a quick glance at the clock on the wall behind his head.

Eight minutes and fifty-two seconds, actually, I think to myself.

"Yeah, sorry." I shake my head to further clear away my thoughts.

I sneak a glance at Brendan to my right, clearly dominating his match against another freshman who just joined the team last week. Outwardly he looks calm and composed, but I know on the inside, he is reveling in his success. I want to check on Dougie, too, but he's at the table directly behind me. If I blatantly ignore my move by turning around to see how his match against our coach, Mr. Michowsky, is going, Will might actually reach across this table and strangle me. I turn my attention back to our board and swipe his rook with my bishop, putting his king into checkmate.

"Damnit!" he cries, standing up and slamming his fists against the table.

"Mr. Stephenson!" Mr. Michowsky yells from behind me, "we'll have none of that language, thank you."

"Sorry, sir." He sits back down, dejected.

I sort of feel bad for the guy, a junior in high school who keeps getting schooled at chess by a measly freshman, but I can't help it that, despite his status as captain, he isn't actually *good* at the game.

At the same time, I've been playing chess since my dad first taught me when I was six, which gives me a significant lead over just about every other member of our team, except our coach, of course, and Brendan. He made me teach him the game when we were seven, because, as his seven-year-old self had said, girls can't be better at sports than boys. I don't think he realized at the time that chess isn't *really* a sport, and no matter how hard he practiced, he would never be as good as me. Luckily, as we've gotten older, his competitiveness has worn off some, which makes it easier for him to handle a loss against me. When we were nine, he was so sure he was going to beat me that when he lost, he didn't speak to me for two whole days. We still laugh about how ridiculous he was back then.

The look on Will's face right now tells me there's a whole slew of curse words he'd like to throw at me, but I know he's too nice to ever actually say them out loud.

"Sorry, Will," I say, reaching across the table to shake his hand. I set the pieces back in their original spaces on the board. "Want to go again?"

"I think I'm sufficiently spent on number of ass-whoopings for today, Janelle." He slumps against his chair and puffs his cheeks up, then blows out a heavy sigh.

"That about wraps up today's practice," Mr. Michowsky interrupts. Everyone goes about recording their unofficial scores and taking photos of unfinished games to resume next practice. "Don't forget, we have our first match against St. George's on Wednesday, so no practice. Please be on time for the bus, everyone!"

After we've packed everything away, I grab my bag and join the others shuffling out of the computer lab towards the stairs. I fall into step with Brendan and Dougie just as Mr. Michowsky glides past us.

"Ms. Beckley, Mr. Grant, Mr. Douglas." He tips an imaginary hat to us.

"Bye, coach," Brendan replies.

"See you Wednesday!" Dougie says, waving. "Nell, you need a ride?" he asks as we tromp down the stairs.

"My mom's supposed to pick me up." I pull my phone out of my pocket to check if she's here yet. She isn't, which isn't surprising since I got my punctuality gene from my dad, not her.

We push out the front doors of the school. Dougie's older brother, Lucas, is waiting in his beat-up blue Ford pickup. My mom's silver Honda is noticeably missing.

"You want us to wait?" Brendan asks, shifting his backpack from one shoulder to the other.

"Sure," I reply. I look around the deserted school parking lot, grateful for the company.

"Yo, Artemis, let's go, little bro!" Lucas rolls down his window and yells. Brendan and I laugh.

"Bye, *Artemis,*" Brendan teases.

"Screw you," Dougie replies, punching Brendan in the arm. He turns to me. "See ya tomorrow, Nell." He heads towards the truck, yelling at his brother to never use his real name like that in front of people, even his friends. He slides in and swings the door shut behind him, but we can still hear him berating his brother, who just laughs while he goes off on him.

"So.." Brendan starts awkwardly, shifting back and forth on his feet, unsure of what to say. "Good game today?"

"Yeah," I nod. "Although poor Will, he hasn't won a single match so far this season. I'm kinda worried what he'll do if he doesn't get at least one win this year."

Why are we even talking about this? I wonder. I give him a small smile, hoping he'll snap out of his weirdness.

"Well, he's definitely not gonna win against you anytime soon," he says. The compliment is genuine, but still feels out of place. He keeps shuffling his feet, like he wants to say more. "Although," he goes on, "with a new boyfriend, maybe you'll be too distracted for chess anymore."

He looks down at his feet, refusing to make eye contact.

"What?" I ask, bewildered. I'm about to press him for more; does he think Keith and I are an item? And why would that mean I would quit chess? But just as I'm forming the right words, my mom rounds the corner of the drop-off circle.

"Never mind," he says as she pulls up to the curb. "Forget I said anything. See you tomorrow." He gives me an awkward army salute before turning to hop into the truck next to Dougie, leaving me standing there more confused than ever.

*****

After dinner, I find myself in my bedroom, debating what I should text to Keith.

If I should even text him at all.

Even though he's *not* my boyfriend, despite what Brendan thinks, he *did* ask me to text him, and I feel a sense of obligation to fulfill his wish, even though I haven't decided yet how I feel about his forwardness in asking.

Without having many ideas of what to say, I keep it simple:

Hey.

I figure he's probably busy doing homework, or eating dinner, or having loads of fun doing anything other than texting me, so I set my phone on my desk and grab an old book of Sudoku puzzles off my nightstand to distract myself while I wait for a reply. I flop down onto my twin bed and pick up in the middle of an old game I started a few days ago. I'm filling in a '9' when I hear the telltale sound of Ninja's panting breath outside the door; she pokes her head into my bedroom, pushing the door open wider once she sees me on the bed.

"Come 'ere, girl," I call to her, and hold out my hand. She approaches it happily and pushes her face against my hand, slobbering all over my fingers. "Ew!" I wipe my hand on the back of my shirt and Ninja plops down on the floor.

Content with Ninja close by, I go back to my game. I'm completing the last box of sixes when my phone buzzes from across the room.

I stand and go to the nightstand, reading his text from the lock screen.

Hey you. How was chess practice? You win?

I sit on the floor and lean against the side of my desk.

It was good, I reply. I won against our captain, Will, although he isn't very good, so winning against him isn't that difficult.

I'm sure it takes talent and effort to win a game of chess, regardless of your opponent's abilities, he goes on. I've never actually played, I'm just assuming it's hard because you only ever see smart people playing it in movies.

I smile to myself, because he isn't wrong, and that seemed like a compliment.

We could play sometime. I could teach you, I reply, feeling a bit giddy at the thought.

Just like when I taught Jason, I can't help but think. I shake my head, desperate to shake the thought of him from my memory.

I'd like that. Although you have to go easy on me, since it will be my first time. He follows his text with a wink. My mouth goes dry thinking about the implied innuendo of that statement. I choose to pretend he doesn't mean what it sounds like he means, and send back a thumbs up emoji instead.

Hey, I have to go help my mom with some stuff, but let's meet earlier tomorrow, same time at our usual spot? Don't think I'll make it through the whole day waiting to see your smile again.

My cheeks turn red at the idea that we have a *spot*, and I'm grateful Keith can't see me right now.

Okay, I answer.

Cool, see you then, he replies.

I let my phone drop onto the plush carpet, then I pull my knees into my chest and heave a deep sigh. I'm tempted to text Shelley right now and tell her all about Keith, but I know I should wait to say it in person. I just want her to tell me how proud she is that I'm trying to move on from Jason, even if it's the most painful thing I've gone through.

Well, not quite the *most* painful thing. I shudder at the thought, my fingers twitching for a safety pin just from the memory of it, and I push it back down.

I just need Shelley to tell me that this is a step in the right direction, that everything will be alright.

That everything can just go back to normal.

I look at the time on my phone and tell myself there's only twelve hours, four minutes and twenty-two seconds until our first class of the day together.

I just need to hold out until then.

Tuesday, September 21st
Fall of Freshman Year

After spending the whole bus ride to school deciding exactly how I would tell my friends about Keith, I think I figured out the perfect way to segue into the topic, without sounding rehearsed. Pleased with myself, I don't even bother watching the clock or the door, instead gazing out the window while I wait for them to arrive to first period.

I'm lost in a trance when I hear Shelley and Crystal finally drop down into the seats next to me.

"So, you meet a guy and don't even bother to tell us?" Shelley barks at me. "So much for being besties."

What? How do they already know?

I turn towards them slowly, knowing I'm going to have to dig myself out of this hole, and fast, before Shelley completely turns on me, like she did in eighth grade when Molly Peters didn't invite us to her pool party. Not that this is exactly the same magnitude of betrayal, but the last thing I need is to lose another friend over a guy.

"Where'd you hear that?" I ask. I cycle back through my memory of yesterday; did they see me talking to him in the hallway? Did Brendan and his big mouth get to them first?

"Does it matter?" Shelley retorts. "*You* didn't tell us, and I'm just trying to figure out why." She crosses her arms over her chest, a sour look on her face.

"Carl told us," Crystal jumps in, trying to help diffuse the conversation. Carl is Crystal's brother, older by one year and three days. He's a sophomore like Keith, but I guess I didn't expect him to be friends with Keith, or at the very least, for him to be the type to meddle in other people's business.

"Carl knows?" I ask, flabbergasted.

"Yeah, he and Keith are friends," Crystal answers. "He's been over to the house plenty of times, actually. He seems like a cool guy." She smiles at me with encouragement.

Keith told his friend about me, I think to myself.

On one hand, I sort of feel flattered that Keith talked about me to his friends, even if that notion makes this whole thing much more real than

I thought it was. It's reassuring to know I won't be some secret he keeps, sneaking around behind people's backs.

I've seen how that mistake plays out already.

But on the other hand, now that he's opened up to his friends about me, I'm in big trouble with my own friends, Shelley in particular, for waiting to tell them until they found out from someone else.

"Sorry, Shell," I apologize. I reach over and gently touch her elbow, but she jerks it away. "It wasn't like I was trying to keep it from you or anything. It's all pretty new, we haven't even officially gone out yet." I pick at my fingernails. "Y'know, I was actually really excited to tell you guys about it this morning, now that there's actually something *to* tell you about."

"So tell us about it." She purses her lips, clearly annoyed.

Despite the daggers she's glaring at me, I go on to recount every tiny detail since my first encounter with Keith. Crystal leans in intently, eating up every word, interrupting me periodically to squeal in delight or ask questions.

Although she seems to be listening, I can't help but feel like Shelley's only waiting for me to stop talking so she can stop pretending to care. I try to silence the tiny, scared voice in my head, but it grows louder with each beat of my heart.

Am I going to lose Shelley next?

When the bell rings to end study hall, I take my time packing up and shuffling out the door. I know I only have four minutes and fifty-nine seconds left to get to Geometry on time, but I can't face walking out with Crystal and Shelley. They're headed to Biology without me, anyway, and don't linger at the door to wait.

As I drift through the halls on my way to class, I feel a familiar itch creeping its way into my brain, that dull ache reminding me that the harder I try to regain control of my life, the quicker it slips from my grasp.

I duck into the closest bathroom, checking the stalls. I see feet in two of them and sigh. Guess I'll have to be extra careful this time.

I take the stall second from the last at the end of the row and lock the door behind me. Luckily these bathrooms are some of the few throughout the school that have been updated recently, so the toilets all have lids. I close the lid quietly and sit, digging a safety pin out of the bottom of my cosmetic bag. I let my body take over, my right hand going to work on my left arm, muscle memory guiding the sharp point of the pin in ways that only inflict just enough pain. I try to allow the dull ache in my wrist to quiet the ache in my mind.

Even though she had to hear it from someone else first, I would have thought Shelley would be happy that I'm trying to move past everything that happened with Jason, and the summer. After all, it was her idea in the first place, even if she doesn't really understand the whole story. But her lack of enthusiasm just makes me nervous that the rift between us is only growing.

And after everything I've done, and all the secrets I've kept from her, I guess I really can't blame her.

Tuesday, August 7th
Summer Before Freshman Year

As the car glided along the interstate, Darrell at the wheel, Janelle ignored the third incoming call from Shelley. But no sooner did she send the call to voicemail than a text from her best friend popped up in its place.

Girl, what the hell is up? CALL. ME. BACK.

Janelle swiped the lock screen on her phone to clear the message, but another one filled its spot almost immediately.

My phone is blowin up, Jason is wiggin out, what's goin on??? Stop ignoring me, biotch.

Everything's fine, Janelle replied quickly.

Right. So you just dumped the "love of ur life" for no apparent reason, Shelley texted back. Janelle could hear the venom in her words, even from three states away.

I'm just not into it anymore. Time to move on, she lied.

Janelle watched the three dots appear on her screen as Shelley typed a reply, and then watched as they disappeared when Shelley thought better of it and deleted her response. Janelle let a few more minutes pass without a response, then shut her phone off and stuffed it down into the crack between the seat cushions of the back seat of the car.

"Can you turn the radio up, please?" Janelle asked her parents in the front seat.

Nora glanced back at Janelle from her visor mirror in the passenger's seat, where she was dabbing at the bags under her eyes with some sort of regenerative cream.

"Sure, sweetheart," she replied, cranking the volume button.

"Thanks," Janelle said. She glanced over at her sister, Lauren, asleep against the window with her earbuds in, then settled into her seat, staring out the window as the trees blurred by, wondering what she had done, what things would be like once she got back home.

If things would ever be the same again.

Tuesday, September 21st Fall of Freshman Year

I can feel Tyler's eyes on me during English, but I pretend not to notice, keeping my eyes fixed on the board.

"What happened?" he finally asks, pointing to the edge of the fresh cut poking out from under my wristband.

"What?" I glance down at the spot he's indicating as if I don't already know exactly what he means. "Oh, nothing," I reply. "Neighborhood cat got stuck in the hayloft. Needless to say, he didn't appreciate me picking him up." I give him a closed-mouth smile, hoping this is enough to satisfy his curiosity; luckily he turns back to his work and doesn't push it further. I pull my arms into my lap and tug at the wristband, trying to stretch it enough to prevent further questions.

"You have about ten minutes remaining," Mr. Vogel reminds us as he circulates the room.

Nine minutes and twenty-one seconds, I correct him in my head.

I risk a glance at Shelley across the classroom, but she's absorbed in a conversation with her partner, Michael. I go back to the scene from Romeo and Juliet that Tyler and I are translating into modern English.

If only navigating high school drama was as easy as understanding Shakespeare.

At the end of class, I wave the guys off to lunch without me. Shelley takes off without so much as a glance in my direction. I walk slow this time so I don't arrive before Keith. I linger at the corner, facing the direction he should be coming from. Students stream past me in both directions. The buzz of conversation fills my ears and drowns out the nervous energy bouncing around in my head. At the warning bell, I crack my knuckles and twist my hands together anxiously. The hallway becomes emptier as students file into the various classrooms on all sides of me. I check my watch; one minute and twenty seconds until the final bell will ring. I hold out, not wanting to stand him up. It's only lunch I'm missing, after all. But when the bell finally rings, making me officially late for the second time, I stare down a deserted hallway, Keith nowhere to be seen. Surprisingly disappointed, I turn and head for the cafeteria.

When I get to my table, I slump down in a seat between Crystal and Brendan.

"You okay?" Brendan asks, digging his wallet out of his bag.

"Yeah," I respond slowly, "It's nothing. Just that guy, Keith, I was telling you about."

"Trouble in paradise already?" Shelley asks, finally looking up from her phone. The smirk on her face tells me she's still holding the grudge from this morning.

"Real nice, Shelley." Brendan shoots her a look of disgust and stands up. "Grabbing a drink, anyone want anything? Nell?" He looks down at me.

"I'm good, thanks." I dig around in my bag for my wallet.

"Get me a Sprite, would ya?" Dougie says as Brendan walks away. Brendan turns back and flashes him two thumbs up.

"So what happened?" Crystal asks between nibbles of her turkey sandwich. "I thought you guys had a date after school today."

"We do. Or I thought we did. He was supposed to meet me in the hallway before lunch but he never showed." I pull books and notebooks from my bag and deposit them on the table, rooting around at the bottom of my bag for my wallet.

"I'm sure there's a reason," Crystal reassures me, patting my shoulder.

"Yeah," Dougie chimes in. "That dude would be an idiot to blow you off."

I give them both a weak smile. "Thanks guys." As my hand closes around my wallet, I feel a buzz from the front of my backpack. I pull out my phone and sure enough, there's a text from Keith, explaining he got stuck finishing a test and is sorry he missed me. I feel a small, unexpected smile creeping out from the corners of my lips.

"That him?" Crystal asks.

"Yeah," I reply. "We're good."

"Crisis averted," Shelley snorts and my smile fades.

I might know what happened to keep Keith from meeting me, but I find myself struggling to wrap my head around Shelley's attitude. I know she's mad I didn't tell her about Keith, but does my slip-up warrant such a snarky, cold shoulder?

Or is this really about the bigger secret I've been keeping from her, keeping from everyone? I know I haven't let it go yet, but has she? And if she won't let it go, does that mean she'll keep acting this way forever? Until I tell her the truth?

Because if that's the case, I don't know which is worse: my best friend hating my guts for not confiding in her, or hating my guts for knowing the truth of what I really did.

*****

The rest of the day goes by in a blur, hurtling me closer and closer to my first official date since my break-up with Jason. I can feel myself growing more and more anxious the closer it gets.

This is good, I remind myself. *Baby steps towards moving on.*

When the final bell rings, I grab my History textbook off the desk, slide out of my chair, throw my backpack on, and slip out of the classroom. I head to my locker, twirling the lock effortlessly, it's *13-4-22* combo setting it free, opening with a click. I slide my textbook inside, pausing for a moment on the picture of Shelley and me taped inside the door. It's a photo of us at the lake together the summer before eighth grade. We're both holding ice cream cones, our arms slung around each other, laughing as the ice cream drips down our hands. The pure joy on our faces is the reason why it's one of my all-time favorite photos of us.

"Hey-oh," Brendan says in my ear. I jump and slam the locker closed. "Sorry," he apologizes. "Didn't mean to scare you."

"No, it's okay," I reply. "What's up?" I click the lock shut and spin it a few times to reset the combo, preventing anyone from pulling it open again.

"Just seeing what you're doing today." He throws his arm around my shoulder as we walk down the hallway towards the school exits. "Dougie and I are headed to Main Street to check out that new vintage arcade. I think Will and a few others are gonna be there. You in?" he asks.

"I have that date with Keith, remember?" I remind him.

"Oh, right," he says.

I stop at the split in the hallway. "I'm actually supposed to meet him in the student lot. But have fun! Let me know how it is."

"Yeah, definitely," he nods. "You too," he adds as an afterthought. "See ya, Nell." He stands there, staring at me.

"Bye..." I trail off, finally breaking eye contact to turn and walk away.

When I get out to the student lot, I stop and look around. Some students mill about near the doors in clumps; others are getting into cars and driving off. Keith told me to meet him here, but didn't actually tell me *where* to meet him. I feel my throat tighten as I begin to panic, but just as I'm about to abort the mission, turn, and run, I hear him behind me.

"Hey."

I turn and he's standing there smiling at me.

"Hi! I was just about to text you," I stutter.

"You ready to go?" he asks.

I nod, my head bouncing like a bobble head.

"Yo Keith!" We both turn to see where the voice came from: a tall, lanky blonde guy wearing a Ronaldo jersey, sitting on the low wall that separates the parking lot from the sidewalk. He's got his arm draped around a brunette in a cheerleader's uniform and several other guys and girls are clustered near him. I notice Carl in the group. As a reflex, I wave to him, but quickly drop my hand when I realize everyone's staring at me.

"Don't have too much fun!" the Ronaldo guy yells to Keith, which sets off laughter among the group. Keith rolls his eyes and shakes his head.

"Friend of yours?" I ask, nervously.

"Ah, don't worry about Garrett, he's harmless. C'mon." He looks down at my hands, clenched in fists against my legs. He takes my left in his right, my palm falling open into his, and pulls me away from his friends towards the parking lot. His touch sends an electric shock up my arm.

"I dunno about you, but I'm ready for some ice cream," he says as we walk. He's still holding my hand as we weave through students and cars exiting the lot. "My last class was Chem and it was brutal."

I just nod, too nervous to speak.

When we approach a black Mini Cooper, he drops my hand and fishes around in his pocket for his keys. He clicks the unlock button twice and pops the trunk, tossing his backpack in. He reaches out for mine and I slip it off my shoulders and pass it to him. He nestles it in the trunk next to his.

He heads to the driver's side door, opening it and sliding into the driver's seat. I go around to the passenger's side door and open it, hesitating a moment before easing myself into the seat next to him. He turns the key in the ignition and the car blares to life, a Blink-182 song blasting through the speakers.

"You can mess with the radio and find something you like," he tells me, turning the volume down so he doesn't have to shout.

"I like this band," I tell him.

"That's awesome," he says. He backs the car out of the parking space and steers towards the school gates. "This is my favorite band."

He eases the car out onto the main road, then rolls his window down to let in some fresh fall air. I roll my side down, too.

“So what other bands do you like?” he asks as we drive along. I rattle off a list of bands in alphabetical order, from most favorite to least favorite.

“Wow, that’s quite a list,” he says, chuckling. I blush at my inability to stop rambling when I’m around him, unsure what to make of my nervousness.

“My cousin is actually the guitarist in a band. He lives in New Jersey. They aren’t famous or anything, but he keeps me in the loop about other up-and-coming bands in the area,” I explain. “We go to a lot of shows together, too, so I get to hear a lot of different types of music.” I realize I’m rambling again, so I clamp my mouth shut to keep from saying anything more.

“Okay, I’m totally jealous,” he tells me. “I’ve always wanted to be in a band, but I don’t have a musical bone in my body.” As he drives, he taps his fingers on the steering wheel in time to the music.

“Your fingers seem to disagree with you,” I say with a sly smile. “But I know what you mean. I used to take piano lessons,” I tell him. “But I was deathly afraid of my teacher, so I quit.”

He laughs loudly. "You're full of surprises, aren't you?" he asks.

I bite my lip and look away, hoping he never finds out what "surprises" truly lurk beneath my surface. I stare out the window at the trees as they whiz by, their bright autumn leaves blurring together into a fiery streak. They remind me of an inferno burning out of control. Not unlike the one I feel raging within me. I just hope I can keep my secrets buried deep enough so I don't get engulfed in my own flames.

Eighteen minutes and two seconds later, we pull into the parking lot of the Swirly Cone. Keith kills the engine and we step out onto the gravel.

"I just need to grab my wallet out of my backpack," I tell him.

"For what?" He cocks his head. "This is a date, remember?"

I blush. He clicks his key fob once and the car lets out a beep to signal it's locked. We head to the order window and scan the menu.

"So here's the million-dollar question," he says while we wait for the family ahead of us to order. "Are you a cone or a cup kinda girl? Me, I'm a waffle cone guy myself." He folds his arms over his chest and turns his head towards me, waiting for my reply.

"I used to eat cones," I start, "but once I discovered the hard shell this place sells, I traded sides real fast. You can get it on the cone, sure, but the cup holds more of the shell. I like to let it harden around the sides of the cup and eat it last. It's a wall of pure chocolate-y goodness." I tell myself to stop rambling, and instead lick my lips and rub my stomach for effect, hoping that my blathering hasn't been too annoying so far. Talking with Jason, even in the beginning, never felt this uncomfortable.

Give it a chance, I remind myself.

Keith cups his chin and nods his head, like he's deep in thought. He motions to the cashier as we step up to the counter to order.

"Ladies first," he tells me. I order a cup of mint chocolate chip ice cream with extra hard shell. He orders a cup of rocky road with hard shell.

"I thought you were a waffle cone guy?" I ask, nudging him in the ribs with my elbow.

"That was a pretty hard sell you made back there. It was the belly-rubbing that got me in the end, I think." He laughs and nudges me back. He hands the cashier a twenty, dropping a couple dollars in the tip jar when she passes him his change.

We take our cups of ice cream, find a picnic table under the overhang, and dig in.

"So I just eat around the wall, right? Save it for last?" He motions with his spoon.

"I mean, if you want to do it *right*," I say, eyebrows raised teasingly. I eat another spoonful, aware of him watching me. "Do you always watch your dates eat with this much intensity?" I ask uncomfortably.

He chuckles. "Sorry. Didn't mean to turn stalker on you. You're just cute when you eat. I mean, you're cute all the time." Now he's the one who blushes. "I'm just gonna shut up now." He looks away from me and runs his hand through his hair.

"You're sweet," I reply, and gesture to my cup of ice cream. "Just like this ice cream. There, now we both said something embarrassing." I crack a smile and he laughs, looking up at me.

"You just have a little something…" He reaches over with his thumb and wipes at the corner of my mouth. His thumb traces the edge of my lip, lingering for a moment before pulling away.

He stares at me intently, his eyes flitting back and forth from my mouth to my eyes. I recognize that look, from a night I hoped never to remember. That look is a reminder that something as simple as a kiss can turn everything all wrong. I break his gaze and look back down at my ice cream, counting the seconds until the moment passes.

The car ride home is quiet as I lose myself in thought. Keith fiddles with the radio and clears his throat several times, trying to draw me back to the present to no avail.

I can't get that look out of my head.

I can't erase the memory of what it means.

"So this was fun," Keith says, interrupting the silence as he shifts the car into park at the top of my steep driveway. My heart begins thumping harder in my chest at his words, so familiar to that night, but I tell myself to calm down. It's a different night. A different car. A different boy.

"Walk you to the door?" he continues, further reassuring me that Keith is nothing like *him*.

I nod slowly. "Sure. Thanks."

He pops the trunk and steps out of the car. I open my door and follow. His fingers graze mine as he passes me my backpack. I reel and pull away.

We start down the winding driveway slowly. His hand brushes mine as we walk and I wonder for a minute whether he's trying to hold my hand or not. Jason was always forward about holding my hand anywhere we went, never hesitating to grab me and show the world I was his.

Stop it, I tell myself.

We get to my porch steps and I pause, turning back to him to signal this is as far as I'll let him.

"So, I hope we can do this again sometime?" He looks at me, his eyebrows raised, hopeful.

"Yeah," I tell him.

"Soon?" he continues.

"Okay." I nod.

He smiles at me. "Cool." He stares me down with dark, smoldering eyes.

"Well, goodnight," I say as I sling my bag over my right shoulder. He holds my gaze, letting me be the one to make the first move. Instead, I slide my hands into my pockets and take a tiny step back. I try to ignore the disappointment on his face.

"Night," he replies. "Text me later, 'kay?"

"Okay." I pull my house key out of my pocket and let myself in. Keith lingers at the bottom of the porch steps, so I give him a tiny wave before gently clicking the front door shut.

As I set my bag down on the bench near the front door, my phone dings with a notification. I slip it from my bag to see it's Instagram.

Probably Brendan, I think as I open the app. Sure enough, he's tagged me in some random parody video of two guys pretending to be Kylie and Kendall Jenner. I roll my eyes but double-tap to "like" the post anyway.

Unable to resist, I find myself swiping out of my notifications and back to my newsfeed, scrolling for any signs of Jason. After a few flicks of my wrist, I come up on his latest post. He's in Bethany's front yard; I recognize the old tire swing from when we were little. He has her in his arms and the ground around them is littered with rose petals that spell *Homecoming?*

I feel bile rise in my throat as I quickly exit the app, grabbing onto the wall to steady myself.

Without fully realizing what I'm doing, or why, I turn back to the front door and bolt out into the night, hoping I'm not too late.

"Wait!" I call after Keith, sprinting back up the driveway.

He's just getting back into his car, but turns at the sound of my voice. I hustle even harder the last few steps until I reach him.

"Everything okay?" he asks.

"Yes," I exhale, slightly out of breath. "I just forgot something."

Before I can stop myself, or really think it through, I grab his collar and pull his face down to mine, pressing our lips together. He pulls back a moment, shocked, before grabbing my face in both his hands and pulling me back into him.

As I let him kiss me, my heart beats wildly in my chest at what I swore I wouldn't do again. My head spins as I lose control, a sense of deja vu washing over me, a familiar thought clawing its way to the surface of my brain. I put every ounce of energy I have into forcing it back down again, but still, it lingers.

Take that, Jason.

Friday, September 24th
Fall of Freshman Year

It's been two days, nineteen hours, and six seconds since my date with Keith, and while I've successfully avoided seeing him at school since, I've also not-so-successfully avoided the reality that I let myself get swept away with my emotions again, that I let jealousy, and insecurity, and anger get the best of me again.

I kissed someone, someone who isn't Jason, when I promised myself I wouldn't do that again, and while this time I know I don't have to keep it a secret, that it isn't the same as last time, it still feels like I did it for all the wrong reasons. And underneath the tangle of emotions I've been feeling since Tuesday, since the summer, really, I feel *his* name lurking somewhere deep in my thoughts, begging to be said, my brain desperate to know what he's doing right now, what he's thinking.

If he's thinking of me.

If he even remembers my name.

If he lays awake at night wondering what happened to me, the way I lay awake trying not to remember what we did.

I shake away the dark thoughts that threaten to pull me down a rabbit hole of misery and go back to stapling the packets Mr. Vogel let me stay after class to help him assemble.

"Thanks, Janelle," he says as the late bell rings. "I think that's good for today."

I lay the final packet on top of the pile and pass them over to him with a weak smile. "Are you sure there isn't anything else I can help you with?" I ask, hopeful.

"Really appreciate it, Janelle, but I think you ought to get to your next class," he replies, taking the papers from me.

"It's just lunch," I shrug. I'd gladly skip a meal if it meant avoiding any awkward run-ins with Keith, run-ins where I'll be forced to explain myself and why I'm dodging him when he's been nothing but nice.

Run-ins where I'm forced to own up to everything I've done.

"Most important class of the day, then," Mr. Vogel laughs, scribbling his signature on a late slip and handing it over. I give him a weak smile and begrudgingly reach out and take it, the paper crinkling in my firm grasp.

As I trudge down the empty hallway, struggling with my thoughts, I want badly to duck into the nearest bathroom, but my growling stomach pushes me onwards. It's easier not to dwell on any of this, anyway, just go back to pretending every move I make isn't because of Jason, that everything I think and do isn't because of what happened. That every dark thought I have isn't because of seeing him happy with someone else.

Someone who isn't me.

But that would also mean I have to pretend that Keith is the answer to my problems, that moving on is important enough that I can just pretend I feel something for him. And the worst part is, it's not even Keith's fault. I know he's a good guy, I could tell the first time I met him. No bad boy would willingly out himself as a Shakespeare nerd, I'm sure of it. He's done everything right, texted me to ask how my day is going, texted just to say hi and tell me that he's thinking of me. I know Keith would never treat me badly, the way *he* did. A kiss can just be a kiss. It can be innocent. It doesn't have to be anything more. Maybe we can just leave it at that.

Except that kind of thinking is exactly what got you into this whole mess in the first place, some dark part of my brain interrupts me, ruining any moment of hopefulness I might have had.

As I approach the cafeteria doors, I try to shove the thought back down, locking it away again, biting my lip in fear as a way to silence the painful thought with real pain, tasting the metallic tang on my tongue as the skin splits, hoping it's enough to keep that part of me satisfied, to keep it silent.

Because I know there's a very real possibility that part of me might eventually break free again, for real this time, to spill my secret to everyone. And the idea of what might happen if everyone found out the truth scares me to death.

I know I've gotten pretty good at pretending lately, but when I finally approach my friends at our table, my face immediately gives me away when I notice Shelley isn't there.

"Where's Shell?" I ask as I sit down in between Crystal and Dougie.

"She said something about meeting in the band room during lunch today," Crystal informs me as she stirs a cold cup of Ramen Noodles.

"Oh," is my only reply. Ever since she got picked for first chair last week, Shelley's barely been around, spending most of her free time outside of class with her new friends from band. I can't help but feel like she's just using it as an excuse not to be around me.

"You getting school lunch today?" Brendan asks as he gets up from the table. "I'll save you a spot in line." He lingers, waiting for my answer.

"No. I'm not very hungry," I lie. He hesitates for a moment, then shrugs and walks away.

I zone out as my friends chatter around me. I feel an emptiness inside me that's more than just my hungry stomach grumbling, an emptiness growing within me where my best friend should be. I haven't had a moment alone with her since school started, and it seems harder and harder these days to pin her down at all. I need that one-on-one we used to have, to get her advice about Keith, about whether I'm being too hard on him or not, to know if I should just give it a real shot with him or not.

To finally tell her everything from the summer.

To come clean.

I need her to notice that I'm not okay, and to help make me okay. I need her in so many ways.

I'm just worried she no longer needs me.

Thursday, August 16th
Summer Before Freshman Year

"Sweetheart, dinner in five, okay? I'm making your favorite, chicken quesadillas," Nora called from the kitchen to where Janelle sat slumped on the couch.

"That's not my favorite anymore, mom," Janelle grumbled, swiping through her various social media newsfeeds.

"Everything okay?" Nora stood at the threshold of the living room, spatula in hand, a worried look crinkled on her face.

"I'm fine, mom," Janelle replied, not looking up from her phone.

"I know breakups are hard, sweetie, but you'll get through it and move on. You'll see. It isn't the end of the world, you know." Nora gave her younger daughter a pitying look before turning back to the kitchen to finish preparing what she hoped would be a comfort meal.

"Whatever," Janelle mumbled under her breath.

She stopped scrolling when she came up on a photo from Shelley, posted earlier that afternoon.

Beach day with my bestie! the caption read. Shelley and Bethany's smiling faces stared back from the photo, picture-perfect on a sparkling beach somewhere in New Jersey, smiles plastered on their faces, their arms linked.

In a matter of days, Bethany had replaced Janelle in more ways than one. As Jason's girlfriend, and now, apparently, as Shelley's best friend.

As Janelle stared at the photo, she couldn't help but wonder if Shelley would have room in her life for *two* best friends. And if she didn't, and Bethany was in, did that mean Janelle was out?

Saturday, September 25th Fall of Freshman Year

As much as I'm *not* looking forward to a weekend with my sister and her boyfriend, as I watch them pull up in Brett's shiny, red Mustang, I hope it at least provides a distraction from everything going on in my life. If nothing else, I know I can at least count on my older sister to monopolize the conversation all night, going on about her fabulous new life as a college student living in the big city.

If you can even call Bethlehem a big city, anyway. I'll never understand why she turned down a full ride to Drexel and the chance at being in the heart of Philadelphia.

Oh wait, I remind myself as I watch Brett climb out of his convertible, *that's why.*

"Janelle, come out and greet your sister," my mom tells me as she glides past me where I'm crouched in the window seat.

"No thanks," I mumble as she passes, my words ignored in the wake of her excitement at her pride and joy being home for the weekend. I go back to my game of virtual chess, tapping the screen of my iPad to put the anonymous opponent on the other end of the screen in check.

I glance up periodically to check on the scene unfolding in the driveway, my mom fawning all over Lauren and Brett, my dad standing stoically off to the side, holding the bags. Sighing, I tip my king in defeat, apologizing to my unknown adversary, then drag myself out to rescue my father.

"So how's the first semester going?" my mom chirps over dinner later that night.

"Oh, it's been so much fun," Lauren starts. "Classes are great, my professors are so cool, and our apartment is just the most adorable little thing." She squeezes Brett's bicep and squeals, and I want to gag.

"Emphasis on little," I say under my breath.

Lauren gives me a look, but continues on. "I've also met a ton of new people. Everyone is just so different from the people in this town. So much more open-minded." She breaks off a tiny piece of her dinner roll and pops it into her mouth.

"That's so great, sweetheart," my mom gushes. "Isn't it, Darrell?" She turns to my dad, his mouth full of porkchop.

"Mmmhmm," he says, nodding.

"I wish your sister would meet some new people," my mom adds as if I'm not sitting right next to her. "Break out of her shell a little. Although she does have a few good ones. And that Brendan friend of hers gets cuter and cuter every time I see him."

"Oh my god, mom," I say in between bites of baked potato.

"Well, you *are* single now, aren't you, Nell?" my sister asks innocently, as if she doesn't already know the answer. "Might be time to get back out there, explore new possibilities."

My mother nods in agreement. My dad and Brett continue eating, saying nothing. I almost tell them about my date with Keith, but think better of it at the last minute.

"Why are we talking about this?" I say instead. "My friends are fine, and I don't need a boyfriend." I drop my fork against my plate with a loud *clink.*

"We were just making conversation," Lauren says. "Don't need to get all huffy. Speaking of your friends, how's Shelley these days? I'm surprised she isn't here tonight, actually," she adds as she takes a sip of her drink. She holds the glass daintily, with her pinky up, like she's some sort of aristocrat drinking wine instead of sparkling juice. "You two were inseparable in middle school. She was over practically every weekend. Although high school changes things, doesn't it?" She turns to me, her blue eyes glinting, although I can't tell if it's on purpose, or just a reflection of the ceiling light.

"You know, Shelley hasn't been over to the house since school started, now that you mention it," my mom interjects before I can reply.

My sister sets her glass down on the table, a smirk washing over her face. "What, did you dump her, too?" she asks, picking at her cuticles.

I feel my face grow hot with anger, my fingers clenching into fists.

"No," I say, holding back a snarl, "she's just been busy is all."

My sister shrugs and everyone goes back to their food. In the momentary silence that follows, I can't help but worry that's *not* all it is. Eventually, the conversation moves on to other topics, but I tune them out, wondering why I ever thought my sister being here was a good idea.

All she's ever done is put me down and cause me trouble, even when we were younger. I guess I shouldn't be surprised that tonight isn't any different, especially considering the last real conversation we had, however brief it was. After the position I put her in that night, I guess it's only fair that I'm at the receiving end of her cruelty.

But I'd still rather deal with her shit for the rest of my life than ever tell her the truth about what I did that night.

Tuesday, August 7th
Summer Before Freshman Year

"Lauren, honey, let's go," Nora called up the flight of stairs. "I swear, that girl is never on time." She gave Janelle an exasperated look, but Janelle just shrugged in response.

"You're just realizing this, mom?" Janelle asked, suppressing a yawn. She hadn't slept a wink since stumbling in earlier this morning. She prayed her parents couldn't tell how out of it she was.

"The girl was late to her own birth, after all," Darrell continued, recalling the almost two-week delay in Lauren's arrival as a newborn.

"I'm coming, I'm coming!" Lauren yelled as she bounded down the stairs. "Geez, you can't be five minutes late in this family, can you?" She pushed past her family towards the door. "*Well*, are we going then?" She gestured with both hands as if *she* was the one who'd been waiting all morning for the rest of the family to get on the road back home and away from their beach house vacation, their last family vacation before Lauren left for college and everything changed.

Janelle realized with a pang that, thanks to her, thanks to what she did last night, things already *had* changed, even if no one but her knew it yet.

"Yes, yes, let's go," her dad said, shuffling everyone out the door and into the car. "I'd like to get going before traffic gets bad." He turned the key in the ignition, the car humming to life.

"Darrell, did you check the kitchen? I can't remember if we emptied the fridge or not," Nora asked as she clicked her seatbelt in place.

Darrell sighed. "I did, but now of course I'll need to go back and check again," he said in slight frustration, turning the car off and stepping back out of the car.

"I'm sorry, dear. I'll come with you," Nora said sympathetically, following him back up the porch steps into the house.

"Remember what I said about last night," Lauren hissed across the seat to Janelle once their parents were out of earshot. "I'm serious."

"It's not a big deal," Janelle assured her sister. "It's not like anything happened, anyway." She bit her lip and hoped Lauren couldn't see the fear written on her face.

"I honestly don't care what stupid antics you got up to with a bunch of losers on the beach," Lauren said, flicking her shiny light brown hair off her shoulders and sweeping it up into a messy bun. "But mom and dad can*not* find out that I left you there alone. They would legit kill me, and I am *not* having that right before I leave for school."

She pulled out her phone, signaling the end to the conversation and no doubt going back to texting Brett, which she'd done just about the entire vacation. Janelle gave her sister a small nod before turning away, staring out the window as she waited for her parents to return.

When they did, and her dad finally pulled out of the driveway, all Janelle could do was watch the beach house, and the beach somewhere behind it, get smaller and smaller, hoping that with each mile she physically put between herself and last night, the further away in her mind she would get from the memory of what she'd done.

Monday, September 27th
Fall of Freshman Year

After a tortuous weekend of pretending to care about anything my sister had to say, and an uncomfortable morning study hall class where I had to listen to Shelley gloat about her new friends in band, I'm glad to finally be in Geometry class. While it was a little rough at first, being the only freshman in what's an otherwise sophomore and junior class- with one senior thrown in the mix who couldn't pass it the first time around- has been a refreshing change from all the other classes I have throughout the day. As much as I enjoy having friends in class with me, at least by the time I get to Geometry, I know I'll have a bit of quiet to just focus on my schoolwork without having to deal with any gossip of the day or reminders of my mistakes.

At least, that's what I thought, anyway.

"I told him he would regret dating a freshman," I hear Megan's voice behind me as I try to solve the area of a trapezoid. "Look at the way she dresses. That should have been a clue right away," she snorts.

I glance to my left, where my classmate, Phillip, and his girlfriend, Rachel, are playing with each other's hair, then to my right, where the sophomore class president, Billy, is scribbling furiously in his math notebook. Okay, so she *is* talking about me.

"Do you think you guys will get back together now?" I hear her best friend, Autumn, ask. I turn my head back slightly and risk a quick peek behind me.

"What are you looking at, nerd?" She practically yells at me, and Autumn giggles. I swivel my head quickly back to the front of the classroom, but not before catching a good look at their faces. I only knew them by name until now, having avoided eye contact with them since the first day of school when they made fun of me for being the only freshman in class. But as I take notice of their matching cheerleader uniforms and their shiny hair, Autumn's brunette and Megan's an unnatural platinum blonde, I realize I've seen them outside of class before, hanging out with Keith's posse in the parking lot after school when we left for our date.

All this time I've been sitting in the same class as Keith's ex-girlfriend and I didn't even know it.

*****

When my phone buzzes against my leg during English, I'm in the middle of rereading the same page of Romeo and Juliet for the third time, no closer to finishing the essay portion of my test than I was five minutes and thirteen seconds ago. I look up to check Mr. Vogel isn't looking and slip my phone out of my pocket, welcoming the distraction until I see who the text is from.

You gonna avoid me forever? Keith's words read.

My thumbs hover over the screen, contemplating a response. I know I owe him at least that much, after ignoring his texts and calls all weekend, and dodging him at school ever since our date on Tuesday, but I can't find a way to make sense enough of my thoughts to explain to him all that I'm going through. Instead of answering, I turn my phone on silent and slide it back into my pocket. I let out an audible sigh and turn back to my test.

"You okay?" Tyler leans over and whispers. I glance up at Mr. Vogel's desk, where he's helping one of my classmate's with their own test.

"Yeah, I'm good," I reply. "I'm just stuck on this."

"Janelle Beckley, stuck on a test? Man, there must be something *really* wrong with you." Tyler chuckles at his joke and goes back to his test. I stare down at the page, considering how much truth there is to his words.

The bell rings twenty-one minutes and four seconds later and I turn my test over to Mr. Vogel, praying for an A and knowing at best it's probably B- work I've turned in. Dejected, I shuffle out of the classroom and down the hallway to lunch, prepared to step into the nearest bathroom and stay there until the late bell rings, but Brendan and Dougie catch up with me before I can slip away. Brendan slings his arm over my shoulder, falling into slow step with me.

"Was it just me, or was that test way easier than all of Vogel's other tests so far this year?" Brendan asks as we walk.

"You sit directly next to Courtney Navid, who just happens to have the highest GPA in the whole freshman class. Of course it was easy for you," Dougie accuses.

"Hey, I resent that," Brendan replies. "I just happen to know my R and J is all."

As we drift down the hallway together, I zone out, pretending to listen as Brendan switches gears, droning on about the new water slide his parents just installed at the camp they run.

"Why would they install a water slide now, right when the weather is turning? It's not like we can even take advantage of it," Dougie complains.

"They always make improvements during the off-season, so everything is ready to go for next summer. You guys have been my friends for how long?" Brendan asks. "You know this already. Tell him, Nell."

"Mmmhmm," I reply, his words barely registering.

As we round the corner of the hallway, I spot Keith walking towards us, laughing at something his friend is saying.

"Hey, I'll catch up with you guys, okay?" I tell my friends. They nod and continue on without me. I slow my pace, lingering by the wall as Keith gets closer. We make eye contact and he turns to his friend, giving him a fist bump before splitting off towards me.

"Hey," I start.

"Hi," he replies, emotionless.

"Look, I'm sorry," I continue, but Keith cuts me off.

"Sorry about what, Janelle? Sorry you kissed me? Sorry you lead me on? Sorry you've been ignoring me all week?" He doesn't yell but I can tell by the way his brown eyes glitter that he's angry.

"I don't get you, Janelle," he goes on. "You act like you're interested, you go on a date with me, hell, you even chase me down at my car to *kiss me*, which was awesome by the way, but totally confusing, because now you're clearly avoiding me. And I don't even know what I did. I feel like I don't know how to act around you."

I feel my own anger building now. "Well, maybe don't talk about me to your ex-girlfriend, for starters," I snap. "It was really awesome listening to her bad-mouth me to her friend during class today." I dig my fingernails into my palms, hoping the pain will keep me from crying.

Keith sighs, some of his anger leaking out with his breath. "Look, I'm sorry about Megan. She can be kind of a bitch when she wants something she can't have. You're right, I shouldn't have said anything to her, but I was pissed at you, and she was willing to listen. I didn't know what else to do."

"Yeah," I reply, looking down at my feet, my anger dissipating. "I'm sorry for being crazy. I don't regret kissing you, it's just, I know what kissing leads to, and I panicked. I'm sorry." I look up at him earnestly, not entirely sure what I want him to say in response.

"God, Janelle, it's not like I was gonna try to sleep with you after we've only gone out once." He ruffles his hair in frustration. "Look, I like you and all, and I definitely don't regret kissing you, either, but I feel like I'm walking on eggshells around you and I don't even know why."

He pauses a minute, and a small part of me wonders if I should just tell him, just blurt it out, because he's right, and while none of this is what I wanted to hear, he doesn't deserve any of it. But before I can decide how to form the right words, he goes on. "I'm sorry, I just can't do this." He looks me square in the eye before he adds, "You're just too complicated."

He hikes his backpack further up on his shoulder before he turns and walks away.

As I watch him go, I know he's right.

I just wish I knew how to uncomplicate my life.

Friday, October 1st
Fall of Freshman Year

I'm picking at one of the self-inflicted scabs on my inner forearm when I hear Shelley's laugh bounce off the walls as she and Crystal enter the classroom. I hurriedly yank the sleeve of my shirt down, covering up the evidence of last night's losing battle with my thoughts, a battle I seem to be losing more and more these days.

"So where is he taking you?" Crystal asks as she slides into the desk to my right. Shelley, who normally sits to my left, putting me at the center of our threesome, takes the seat on Crystal's other side, away from me. I try not to let it bother me, but the more she brushes me off, the worse it feels. I should be used to her cold shoulder by now but I can't help wishing we could just forget everything that's changed between us and go back to the way things were. But that probably means I have to own up to everything, to tell her the truth, and I haven't decided if it's worth it yet. I can't help wondering if the truth would even actually get me my best friend back.

"He won't tell me," Shelley replies, ignoring me and continuing her end of the conversation. "Said it's a surprise." She beams at Crystal and flicks her glossy blonde hair off her shoulder. I notice the length looks shorter than usual, with more layers. I pretend not to notice that she obviously went to the salon without me, even though we've been getting our hair cut together since we were eight.

"Well, I'm sure it will be great no matter where you go." Crystal says. She pauses, then looks over at me. "We should all go out together sometime, the three of us, and our boyfriends."

"Wait, you and Steve are a couple now?" I ask, confused. "I thought you just went out a few times so far?"

Shelley had dropped hints that she and Steve Harrison, the junior from band that her friend, Maggie, had introduced her to, were dating, but from the little bit of information I'd gleaned from her bragging, they weren't an official item yet.

"Made it official a week ago," Shelley informs me. She digs her Biology notebook out of her bag, content on ending the conversation there, without so much as another word about her new relationship. I'm trying to find the right words to keep her talking, but luckily Crystal beats me to it.

"Tell Janelle how it happened." Crystal's blue eyes sparkle with excitement.

"What, did he make a big production or something?" I'm trying hard to show interest, willing her to let me back on her good side. With our friendship so tense these days, I worry if I've said the right words or if my question will be met with a snarky reply. Or worse, a snort and an eye roll. But if I know one thing about Shelley, it's that she loves to talk about herself.

Apparently it works, because she closes her notebook and swivels in her chair to face us.

"Oh my god, Nell, *totally*," she says, making eye contact, and I feel a happiness spread through me as I recognize the old Shelley surfacing, replacing the imposter that had taken up residence these last few months. She goes on for a few minutes, describing in detail how Steve, with the help of a few band friends, planned this huge romantic gesture to officially ask her to be his girlfriend.

As I listen intently to her recount every tiny detail of his serenade, I pray that with Shelley focused on her own budding romance, she'll be too preoccupied to ask about mine. But her self-absorbed nature only lasts so long before she stops for a breath and finally asks the question I've been avoiding.

"So what about you, how are things between you and Keith going?" Maybe she's just coming down off the high of her new girlfriend status, but for once she seems genuinely interested in my answer. For once since I met Keith, I wish she wasn't.

I suck my lower lip anxiously before answering quietly, "Um, there is no Keith and me."

"Really. Well that didn't last long." As quickly as the old Shelley had surfaced, I feel her slipping back underneath the new, bitchier version just as fast.

"Oh, what happened?" Crystal asks, resting her hand on my arm like a concerned mother.

"It's complicated," I say hesitantly. My eyes dart to Crystal's hand, where only a thin piece of cotton sleeve separates her unpolished fingers from one of my many secrets. Shelley is no longer looking at me. I search for the words to explain what happened with Keith; I even consider going back to August, back to the start of all this, finally letting them in on everything, but Shelley responds before I find my voice.

"Everything seems to be complicated with you these days," she snips, and goes back to her Biology notes.

I know she's right but, considering she only knows half the story, her words hardly seem fair.

Would she feel differently if she knew the truth?

Monday, October 4th
Fall of Freshman Year

At practice Monday afternoon, I find myself staring at the chess board in front of me, my mind refusing to make sense of the pieces positioned on their black and white squares, unable to decipher the perfect moves to outmaneuver my opponent. As hard as I try, I can't force out the cluster of thoughts cluttering my mind, making it impossible to concentrate on the game.

Since my last real conversation with Shelley in study hall on Friday, all I can think about is how badly I miss my best friend, and how much I need her on my side again. But I've been racking my brain for the last three days, six hours, twenty-nine minutes, and eleven seconds to determine a way back to the friendship we had, and the only thing I've come up with so far is to just tell her everything, which is completely out of the question.

Just the thought of someone knowing the truth makes me want to scream, or throw up, or both.

I can feel Dougie's eyes burning a hole into the top of my head while my mind is elsewhere. I hastily push one of my pawns forward on the board and he slides in and swipes my remaining bishop, putting me in check.

"Man, I woulda thought you'd see that move coming, Nell," Dougie says, his dark eyebrows arched in surprise.

"Yeah, sorry," I reply, tipping my king over and forfeiting the match. "My head just isn't in it today."

Dougie lets out a frustrated sigh, no doubt disappointed at winning by default, but right now, I just don't care.

With only eleven minutes and forty-one seconds left of practice, there's not enough time to start another round, not that I want to keep playing anyway, so I start packing up the board, flinging the pieces into their box haphazardly.

"You okay?" Dougie asks as he helps me pack up. "You seem a little…" he trails off, searching for the right word. "...Agitated," he settles with.

"Yep, all good," I grumble, "just not feelin' it today."

Once we have all the pieces put away, I take the box to the back of the room, shoving it onto a bookshelf with the extra analog clocks used to time each game.

Dougie makes his way over to Brendan's match, where our teammate, Eddie, has him locked in a game of cat and mouse. I shuffle over as well, standing over Brendan's shoulder and watching as he thwarts every attempt Eddie makes at checkmate. Finally, with only their kings and Eddie's pawn remaining and no viable moves left, the match ends in a stalemate.

"Did anyone finish a game today?" Dougie questions as Brendan begins packing away the board.

"What d'you mean?" Eddie asks, recording his final time in his logbook.

"I mean you guys had a draw, Nell forfeited, Will's over there crying about his match getting cut short because Rob had to leave early..."

"I am not crying!" Will interjects from the other side of the room, where he and Mr. Michowsky are going over his team ranking.

Dougie gives Will a *'yeah, right'* look before he goes on. "Just seems like one of those days where no one played well or even got to finish a game."

"Wait, Nell, you forfeited?" Brendan pauses, the knight in his hand hovering over the open box, waiting to join its mates. "That's not like you." He stares at me, waiting for an explanation.

"Yeah, that's what I thought," Dougie adds.

"It's fine. I'm fine," I lie, grabbing the piece out of his hand and tossing it into the box.

"Yeah, you sure *seem* fine," Brendan eyes me, his sarcastic comment digging deeper than he probably intended. He puts the lid on the box and passes it to Eddie, who carries it off to the bookshelf. "Is this about Keith?"

"Why would it be about Keith? I knew him for like, five seconds," I say as I fiddle with the edge of my sleeve.

"True." He's still staring at me, trying to read my thoughts. I look away, hoping he just drops it. "It's about Jason, isn't it?" he tries again.

"What?" I reply, looking back at him. "What makes you say that?"

With Brendan's eyes on me, I silently hope he doesn't connect the dots all the way back to the summer, to what started all of this.

"I dunno, Nell, maybe because it's obvious to anyone with eyes that, even though *you* dumped *him,* you're clearly not over it," he says slowly.

"Plus it can't be easy having to share your friends with him and all," Dougie chimes in.

"And what about Bethany?" Brendan doesn't let up. "What kind of heartless bitch does that to her so-called friend?"

"I know, right? And why would Jason even want to date someone who treats her friend like that? Not to mention that Bethany is nothing compared to Janelle," Dougie replies. "Jason basically settled for the runner-up."

While I appreciate him sticking up for me, Dougie is wrong. I don't think Bethany would ever do to Jason what I did. Somehow I feel like that makes her a better girlfriend than I ever was.

"Those two deserve each other, that's for sure," Brendan continues.

"You're right," I snap. "Thanks to Jason and Bethany, things have been pretty miserable since school started. Is that what you wanted to hear?" I huff, and storm off towards the door.

"Janelle…" Brendan starts, but I'm already out of the room, refusing to discuss it any further.

*****

As I pretend to work on my poetry assignment later that night, I can't stop thinking about Brendan and Dougie's conversation at practice. It was true breaking up with Jason made things instantly tense with my other friends; shared custody definitely isn't any easier even when everyone involved is still in high school. And yeah, Brendan wasn't wrong, dating your friend's ex doesn't exactly make you friend of the year. But they were both wrong to imply that this was anyone's fault but my own.

Having given up on my poem completely, I swipe my phone off my desk and settle back in my chair. I scroll through my text message log, hovering over the last text I received from Bethany, mere days after I broke it off with Jason.

Jason n I are together. Wanted u to hear it from me instead of some1 else.

While I appreciate her maturity at coming out and telling me herself (albeit through a text instead of to my face), I don't think I'm *quite* ready to forgive her for breaking girl code just yet. I swipe left and delete the convo history. Eventually we'll need to have it out, but now's not the time.

I keep scrolling until I come to my text history with Jason. I read and reread his final message to me, sent the same August day that I dumped him, just hours after the worst day of my life.

Just tell me what I did wrong.

If only he knew it wasn't what *he* did wrong, it was what *I* did wrong. Out of everyone, didn't he at least deserve to know the real reason we broke up?

I consider calling him, but he'll probably just ignore it. After all, that's what I would do if he dumped me without so much as an excuse. A text seems safer, anyway.

I'm not quite sure how to start so I figure I should just keep it simple. Just a basic *'hey'* to get the ball rolling. If he wants to ignore me, that's fine, but at least he will get the message. Unless he blocked my number, which I suppose is more realistic than anything else.

But if he didn't block my number, maybe I owe him more than just a casual *'hey'*?

Can we talk? I type, then decide it isn't enough, holding down the backspace button to erase it.

Hey, can you call me? I want to explain everything.

I reread the text over and over before hitting send, until I've read it so many times I've talked myself out of it. As much as he deserves the truth, I can't bear to tell it. I delete the text, knowing it makes me a coward, but I'm just not ready to face what I've done.

In fact, the more I contemplate it, the more I'm unsure if I'll ever be ready to face the truth.

Tuesday, August 7th
Summer Before Freshman Year

Janelle waited until they'd gotten about an hour into their drive before digging her phone out of her bag. It had taken her about that long to drum up the courage to do what she was about to, anyway. Although she still wasn't entirely convinced she was ready to do this.

Can't go back in time and change what I've done, she thought to herself. *This is the only way.*

She opened her text messages, ignoring the group texts between Brendan, Dougie, and Tyler, as well as the one between Shelley, Crystal, and Bethany.

Stay focused, she reminded herself. *Just do it, like ripping off a Band-Aid.*

She knew it was going to be much more painful than that, but what other choice did she have? She opened the thread with Jason, ignoring his last message asking if they'd gotten on the road yet, and punched out a new text.

I can't do this anymore.

Before she could talk herself out of it, she hit send and clicked off the phone, holding it tight in her hand while she waited for a reply. She tried to slow the pounding of her heart, taking deep breaths in and out of her nostrils, but it wasn't helping. Finally, a reply came through.

What do u mean? Can't do what?

She had expected push back, for sure, but wasn't entirely sure how Jason was going to react. He seemed confused; maybe her first text wasn't clear enough, so she made sure to spell it out for him with her next one.

I don't want to be your girlfriend anymore.

The words couldn't be further from the truth, but she hit send before she could change her mind, afraid that if she didn't do this, she would end up telling him the truth, instead.

And that was so much worse.

Instead of a reply, her phone started buzzing with an incoming call, Jason's customized ringtone blaring from the tiny iPhone speakers.

"You mind?" Lauren grumbled from the other side of the backseat, where she was curled up inside her sweatshirt's hood.

"Sorry," Janelle said, switching her phone to silent as she let the call continue ringing. No sooner did the call end than another came through. This time, Janelle ignored it, sending it to voicemail. Her phone *pinged* to let her know she had a new voicemail.

Nell, pick up the phone. Another text from Jason came through, but Janelle just swiped to clear it from her screen.

Plz

Don't do this

Nell?

Plz answer me

Nell pick up the phone

He called again, and again Janelle sent it to voicemail. Frustrated with drawing out this already painful task, she typed a quick reply and sent it back.

It's over. Please just accept that. She leaned into her seat, digging her nails into her palms to keep from screaming, or crying.

What happened? What did I do?

Janelle could hear the desperation in his words, and she wanted to call him, to tell him she was wrong, that this wasn't the way it had to be, after all. But she knew there was no other option.

I just don't want to be with you anymore. Just move on.

That's it, she told herself. *Don't say anything else. Don't go round and round, don't let him talk you out of this.*

Nell plz

We can fix this

Just tell me what I did wrong

Janelle cleared the unread texts from her phone and stowed it away in her bag. She chewed on her lip as she watched the trees blur by out the car window, wondering if Jason would ever forgive her.

If she would ever forgive herself.

Thursday, October 7th Fall of Freshman Year

"Janelle, can I speak with you for a minute?" Mr. Vogel asks when the bell rings to end English class. The shuffle of my classmates on their way out the door to lunch almost muffles the seriousness in his voice.

"Sure," I reply, uneasy. I glance over at my friends. "I'll catch up with you at lunch," I tell them, and make my way to the front of the room.

Brendan looks back at me as he makes his way out of the room, Dougie and Tyler chattering beside him. He holds my gaze, concerned, but I shoo him away with the wave of my hand.

"Yes?" I ask Mr. Vogel politely, hovering near his desk. He follows the last stragglers to the door, shutting it behind them softly. I gulp uncomfortably, wondering what this is about.

"I just wanted to see how you're doing, Janelle," Mr. Vogel starts. He walks back towards me and sits at his desk, pulling something from a manila folder. He holds it out in front of me; it's the Romeo and Juliet test we took a few weeks ago. His familiar looping handwriting has scrawled a 'C-' at the top near my name. I stare down at it, the red ink burning into my retinas.

"You seem a little off lately," he continues, "so I just wanted to make sure there wasn't anything going on outside of class that I should be aware of."

When I make no move to take the paper, he sets it down on the desk in front of me. "It's obvious what kind of student you are, so I admit I was a little surprised after grading this test." He looks up at me, waiting for me to explain.

"Um, we all have bad days?" I say, my voice lilting up at the end almost like a question. My fingernails nervously dig into my palms as I wait for him to prod more.

He sighs. "I suppose we do," he says after a beat. "Well, I just hope you know I'm always here if you ever need to talk about anything. My door is always open." He gives me a half smile.

"Thanks, Mr. Vogel. I appreciate that, really." I return the half smile then pull down on the straps of my backpack and scurry out of the room.

I shuffle quickly towards the cafeteria, keeping my head down even though the hallway is mostly deserted. I turn the corner, trying to ignore the fact that this is the same corner where I accidentally "met" Keith twenty days, three minutes, and eight seconds ago.

It's hard to believe how much has changed in just under a month.

I spot a pair of teachers coming at me down the main hall from the office, talking over a stack of papers. I pick up my pace, silently cursing myself for not getting a tardy pass from Mr. Vogel. I duck into the cafeteria right as they look up, narrowly avoiding a detention slip for being in the halls after the bell.

I make a beeline for my lunch table, where Brendan, Dougie, and Tyler are already eating, Dougie's hands gesturing wildly as he talks, his typical Dougie way.

I'm steps away from joining them when Jason appears out of nowhere, cutting me off before I can make it to the safety of my table.

"What the hell, Janelle?" he spits at me. "You couldn't bear to see me happy with someone else so you had to talk shit about me behind my back?" Venom drips from his words.

"What are you talking about?" I ask, generally confused. I glance past his broad shoulders; Brendan, Dougie, and Tyler are looking my way, having picked up on the commotion. Brendan pushes his chair away from the table and stands, waiting to jump in if needed. I turn back to Jason, his green eyes burning a hole in me.

“Did you forget I’m friends with your teammate, Eddie?” he seethes.

It hits me he’s referring to the conversation from Monday’s practice. I think back, trying to remember exactly what I said.

“Maybe watch who’s within earshot before you go bad-mouthing me and my girlfriend to your friends.” He takes a step closer and I swear I can see actual steam coming out of his ears. In an instant, Brendan steps in front of me, shielding me from Jason’s wrath.

“Yo man, back up,” he grunts, pushing Jason back with a slight shove. Jason takes a step towards Brendan and I see his fists clench. His eyes glitter in that way they do when he’s enraged. I’ve only seen it one other time, when he forcibly removed his mom’s abusive ex-boyfriend from his house last spring. I know what that look means, so I brace myself, waiting for him to throw the first punch. I wonder if Brendan can hold his own against Jason, who’s at least a head taller than him, or if Dougie and Tyler will have to jump in. I glance over at Jason’s table, where his friends are watching, and wonder which of them will join in on the fight, and which of them will break it up.

But before I can contemplate how much trouble I'm about to be in for being at the center of this, Jason forces a deep exhale and unclenches his fists. He glares past Brendan right at me.

"Stay the hell away from me and Bethany," he growls. "Both of you." He gives Brendan a look of contempt before finally turning and stomping off to his own table of friends. I watch him go, and lock eyes with Bethany. She turns to Jason as he sits, giving him a hug and rubbing his back in moral support. She glares at me over Jason's shoulder as she consoles him. It takes me a minute before I realize Shelley and Crystal are both staring at me, too, their faces hidden behind several of Jason's friends. They look as if they don't know whether to be scared or disgusted. I feel a small pang deep within me as I realize battle lines have officially been drawn.

"What an ass," Brendan says, interrupting my thoughts. He looks at me with a '*can you believe that guy?*' smirk, waiting for me to agree. But the reality of what just happened has settled in fully, and I snap.

"Stop trying to fight my battles for me!" I practically yell at him. "You're not my boyfriend!"

The smirk on his face instantly disappears and his mouth hangs open for a minute before his lips draw up into a tight line.

"You're right," he begins slowly, "I'm not. You don't have a boyfriend. Remember?" He delivers the words with something more than just frustration, something close to disdain, nodding back over at Jason to make his point.

He turns on his heel and walks back to the table, refusing to look up at me even after he's seated. Tyler fidgets in his chair, his blue eyes darting from me to Brendan to Dougie, unsure where to actually look. Dougie clears his throat and takes a sip of his Gatorade, avoiding eye contact altogether.

Brendan's words hang in the air and I stand there, stunned, for another 10 seconds before I finally storm out of the cafeteria and into the nearest bathroom.

I lock myself in a stall, thrashing around in my bag for the sharpest thing I can find, not even bothering to care anymore who might hear me. My fingers finally close around a brand new tin of safety pins. I yank the lid from the top and safety pins explode in a metal shower, sprinkling the floor around me.

"Hey, you okay?" a voice asks from the other side of the door.

"I'm fine!" I screech, and scramble to snatch up the pins that litter the floor. I see a pair of sandals hover outside the door for a minute, before finally moving away towards the exit. I stuff the extra safety pins back in my bag and wait to hear the definitive *click* of the door closing before I shove my sleeve up past my elbow.

As I scratch at myself, I think about how furious I am with Jason for scolding me in front of everyone, as if I was a child. I think about how furious I am with Bethany, for betraying my friendship and choosing a guy over me. I think about how furious I am with Shelley, and even Crystal, for clearly taking sides. And I think about how furious I am with Brendan, for starting this fight with his big mouth at practice Monday. And more than anything, I think about how furious I am with myself for putting all of this in motion that August night all those weeks ago.

With each stroke of the sharp pin, I let the emotional pain within me leak away. With each drop of blood, I feel my anger and embarrassment ooze out of me. But no matter how good the physical pain feels, I can't seem to release the regret building within me.

I knew I'd eventually pay for what I'd done. I knew it was only a matter of time before my guilt caught up to me.

I just didn't realize that it meant losing everything.

Wednesday, August 15th Summer Before Freshman Year

It had only been 48 hours since Bethany and Jason became an official couple, but every hour that ticked by, each minute that passed, only made Janelle feel worse than the last. She'd hoped the more distance she put between herself and her painful new reality, the easier it would feel, but nothing about this was easy.

Every waking minute was spent thinking about Jason being with Bethany, or missing Jason, reminiscing on the times they had, or thinking about that night, what she did to cause all of this. She'd love to stay in bed and never come out again, but when she hadn't gotten out of bed that entire first day, Nora had come knocking, desperate to pull her daughter from her funk and help her move on with her life.

If only she realized this was about more than just a breakup.

The last thing Janelle wanted was her mom poking around, discovering her dark secrets, so when it seemed Nora would never let her out of her sight again, Janelle had mustered the last ounce of energy she had to at least relocate her suffering to the living room.

"I'll make you some pancakes," Nora said as Janelle slumped down onto the couch.

"Unngh," Janelle mumbled. She flicked on the tv, landing on the last channel her mom had been watching, but was too out of it to bother to change the station. Instead, she stared past the QVC programming, where a woman was modeling a leather handbag, zoning out as her eyes locked onto the wall behind the TV, glazing over as she tried to get her mind to quiet.

Her phone made a noise, reminding her she couldn't actually avoid what was happening. She tentatively turned it over, half-hoping there would be a text from Jason saying he was sorry, that he made a mistake with Bethany and wanted to work it out with her instead.

But then she reminded herself it was *her* fault Jason was even with Bethany, that her actions drove him to it, and she became so despondent, she almost forgot about her phone altogether. But she caught sight of Brendan's name on the screen, and the tiniest glimmer of hope pushed her on.

Hey, heard about J n B, wow is all I can say. Talk about backstabbing. Ur better off w/o both of em. Always here if u wanna talk, never going anywhere xoxo

Although it wasn't the person she really wanted to hear from, and it wasn't exactly what she wanted to hear, it was also exactly what she needed at that moment. Janelle felt the corners of her mouth twitch slightly, desperate to form even the tiniest of smiles. She breathed in the smell of her mother's cooking and sighed.

As long as she had Brendan by her side, maybe things wouldn't be so bad after all.

Friday, October 8th Fall of Freshman Year

"So did you talk to Shelley about Florida yet?" my mom asks me over her famous lasagna dinner the next night.

I dig the tines of my fork into its gooeyness and push it around on my plate. After yesterday's blowout at lunch, I haven't talked to anyone about anything, but I'm not about to tell my mom that.

"She can't go," I lie, knowing even if I drummed up the courage to ask her, there's no way she'd say yes, anyway. "She has some band thing that week."

I shovel a bite of lasagna into my mouth to prevent the scream building inside me from leaking out.

"Oh, I'm sorry to hear that," my mom replies. "Feel free to ask someone else," she says, giving me a small smile and taking a sip of her Chardonnay.

"What about Brendan?" my dad chimes in.

"Darrell, I don't think it would be appropriate bringing a boy with us on a family trip to Florida," she says aloud to the both of us.

"It's not like he's my boyfriend or anything," I blurt out, telling my parents the same thing I reminded Brendan of just yesterday. Although I'm not sure why I'd even want Brendan to go anywhere with me right now, not after what he said yesterday once I uttered those words. I don't even blame him for the way he reacted, but the venom in his eyes is forever burned into my brain, and at this point, I don't even know where we stand.

"Does *he* know that?" my mom asks, raising her eyebrows at me and drawing me back in from my spiraling thoughts.

"What's that supposed to mean?" I set my fork back down on my plate and give her a look, but she just goes back to her dinner, ignoring my question.

"I'm just not comfortable with it, Janelle," she goes on. "You have other girl friends, ask one of them." She looks at me with her *this-conversation-is-done* face.

"It was dad's idea, anyway," I mumble, but she's already moved on to other topics, telling my dad about her plans to re-landscape the backyard.

As I listen to them talk about rock walls and mulch options, I consider my mom's words. *Do* I have other girl friends? Between Bethany betraying me by dating my ex, and Shelley and Crystal essentially ditching me for Jason's posse, as evidenced by the looks they gave me across the lunchroom yesterday, who did that leave?

I'm not even sure Brendan is my friend at this point.

In fact, I'm not sure of anything anymore.

The only thing I know for sure is I do not trust myself to go on another beach vacation alone.

Monday, August 6th
Summer Before Freshman Year

Janelle shook her head, trying to dislodge more than just the water from her ears. For the last fifteen minutes or so, she'd just bobbed on the surfboard Travis had lent her, watching as he rode wave after wave, making it look so easy.

She sighed. She shouldn't be here. Despite what she'd been feeling yesterday, when she saw that picture of Jason at the lake, something about this whole surfing thing just felt off. She bent forward, pressing her bare stomach flat to the board and started paddling back into shore. She only made it a few strokes before Travis floated up next to her.

"Alright, you ready to give it another go?" he asked. He was grinning at her with those sparkly teeth of his, sunlight glinting off them.

Janelle sat up straight on her board. "I dunno," she sighed. "You saw those wipeouts. I don't think I can handle any more embarrassment today." She forced a laugh, trying to shrug off how terribly their lesson had gone.

"Nah," Travis assured her, "you can't expect to get it all in one take. C'mon, give it a few more tries and then we'll call it." He sat up on his own board and looked at her eagerly.

She didn't know why, but the longer she stared back at him, the more she wanted to impress him.

"Okay," she said finally, ignoring her earlier thoughts. "Just a few more times."

"Yes!" Travis pumped his fist in the air. "Okay, remember, when I say go, pop up and get your feet under you as quick as you can. Arms out for balance." He held his own arms out to the sides to demonstrate. "Don't worry about falling."

"Easy for you to say," Janelle teased.

"Hey, I had plenty of my own gnarly wipeouts when I was first learning." Travis slapped at the water, splashing Janelle playfully. She giggled. Travis's gaze shifted past her, towards an incoming wave.

"This is it, paddle! Paddle!" Travis yelled. The smile on Janelle's face vanished and her eyes narrowed, zeroing in on the water in front of her. She paddled as hard as she could, feeling the pull of the undertow as the wave got closer and closer.

"Now!" Travis's voice was almost lost in the rush of water around her, but she heeded his advice and pushed herself up to a standing position. She wobbled ever so slightly, but with her arms out in a slight T formation, she caught herself just in time. She felt the force of the wave propel her forward and her exhausted legs buckled under her, but she pushed the fatigue further down and pressed on.

"I'm doing it!" she shrieked. She rode the wave all the way to the shoreline where she hopped off her board into the ankle-deep water.

"That was so dope!" Travis commended her as he came up beside her. He stood in the shallow water, one hand on his board, and leaned in to give Janelle a one-armed hug.

"Thank you!" Janelle gushed, throwing both arms around Travis's neck and giving in to his hug fully. Travis wound his other arm around her, pulling her close to his chest. She nuzzled her face into his neck and, without thinking, reached up and pulled his face down, pressing her lips to his. His lips had beads of water still clinging to them, and they tasted like a mixture of salt and sunblock. She pulled back slightly to catch her breath, opening her eyes and gazing up into his. Only the eyes staring back into hers weren't the familiar green of Jason's, and she pulled away, realizing what she'd just done.

"Oh my god!" she squealed, her hands slapping over her open mouth. "I can't believe I just did that!"

"Hey, I'm not complaining," Travis replied, smoothing out his tousled blonde locks.

"No," Janelle continued, quietly, "I mean, I have a boyfriend."

Travis shrugged. "He doesn't have to know," he told her. He waded out of the shallow water back onto the sand, surfboard in one hand. He looked back where Janelle stood frozen in embarrassment. "You coming?" he asked.

Janelle let out a deep breath and sloshed through the water, following Travis back up to the pile of shoes and clothes they'd left in the sand. He handed her a blue towel, and wrapped a green one around his waist. Janelle grabbed the towel and stood there, unsure what to do.

"I'm really sorry about that," she finally said.

Travis picked up his left shoe and dug out his phone. "No biggie," he replied, swiping through his phone. "I gotta get your board back to the shop," he continued, eyes still glued to the screen, "but there's this bonfire later tonight, down here on the beach. You should come." He finally looked up at Janelle, his blue eyes burning a hole in her.

After the stunt she just pulled, she should tell him no. She could write off that kiss as being caught up in the moment, just the adrenaline of the day causing a momentary lapse in judgement on her part.

But continuing to hang out with Travis would only bring more trouble.

She was about to decline, tell him thanks but no thanks, but Janelle couldn't stop picturing Jason and their friends, lounging on that picnic table at the lake, laughing without a care in the world, in total disregard of her or her feelings. She swallowed down the guilt and nervousness bubbling within her, ignoring the part of her brain that was screaming '*no,*' and instead let her anger and resentment take over, her next words spilling out of her mouth effortlessly.

"I'd love to."

Tuesday, October 12th
Fall of Freshman Year

It's been five days, four hours, thirty-eight minutes and fourteen seconds since my fight with Brendan and neither one of us has said a word to the other yet. I pretend to work on my Geometry homework at the kitchen table, when really all I'm doing is glancing over at my phone every five seconds, wondering if he will call. Or if I should just call him.

"You okay, Nell?" my mom interrupts the back and forth in my mind, silencing the internal struggle, at least for the moment. She gives me a concerned look, pausing over the fruit salad she's chopping at the counter.

"Huh?" I reply as I look up, still somewhat distracted.

She gestures at me with the knife in her hand. "You seem bothered by something," she says.

I follow her gaze and realize I'm tapping the end of my pencil vigorously against my textbook, unaware it's giving me away. I set the pencil down and pull my hands into my lap.

"It's nothing," I tell her as I clench my fists, grateful she's far enough away not to notice. "This homework is just tough."

I sigh and flip the page in my textbook, a signal that I don't want to talk about it any further. Thankfully, she picks up on it and goes back to her salad.

I'm finally getting into the actual math problem in front of me when my phone buzzes loudly. I jump in my seat and scramble to grab it as it vibrates away from me on the table.

"Hello?" I answer without even checking the caller ID on the screen, hoping it's Brendan.

"Hey Janelle!" It's Carrie, my mom's best friend, and my store manager.

"Oh, hey," I reply, trying to hide the disappointment in my voice. "How are you?"

"Girl, I'd be a ton better if you'd agree to work tomorrow after school," she says. "Pat called out and everyone who isn't already on the schedule is busy. I know it's Wednesday, and you have chess, but you'd really be saving my ass," she pleads.

After ditching practice yesterday, feigning illness, I doubt that excuse will work again tomorrow. A real excuse like having to work would probably go over much better with Will, anyway. I guess the silver lining to actively avoiding my friends is at least I'll get paid this way.

"Of course I will," I tell her.

"Awesome! You rock!" she practically shouts. "Just come in when school's over, as soon as you can. Love you!"

"No worries," I reply. "Love you too."

She hangs up and I click my phone off, setting it back on the table near the edge of my notebook.

"That was Carrie," I tell my mom. "She needs me to work tomorrow so I'll need a ride after school."

"Oh," my mom replies. She's by the stove now, slathering garlic on a loaf of bread she's about to stick in the oven, and she turns around to look at me. "But I thought you had a match tomorrow. Are you sure?"

"She needs me, mom," I say by way of explanation. I know I could have told her no, but Carrie wouldn't have asked if it wasn't dire. I also don't mind letting her be my excuse to get out of having to face Brendan after the things we said to each other.

"Okay," she says, hesitantly. "As long as you're sure." Her gaze lingers on me, so I nod energetically and give her a small smile to satisfy her.

After I finish clearing the dinner dishes, I head into the living room. My parents are out on the back deck sharing a bottle of wine, no doubt being romantic and nauseating. I turn on the TV, intent on drowning out their conversation with any number of shows I've saved to my Netflix queue. I scroll through my list, trying to find something equal parts entertaining and easy to follow. Hard as I try, I still have that lunchroom blow up on my mind, so I search for something mindless. I settle on an episode of Tiny Home Nation, knowing it will still be easy to follow even if I miss some of the dialogue.

As I watch the transformation of a rundown school bus into a beautiful tiny home on the move, I fiddle with my phone, opening various social media apps and scrolling through my friends' feeds. I'm not really sure what I'm hoping to find, but I feel some comfort in seeing their smiling faces again, even if it is through a screen.

Everything that's happened is my fault, so it feels only fair that I'm the one who makes the first move to repair the damage. I want to talk to

Brendan, but I'm not ready to call him. Mending things feels better suited for an in-person conversation, anyways.

Instead, I open the group text with Shelley and Crystal. The looks they gave me at lunch last week are still burned in my mind, and I would do anything to erase them.

Hey, you guys wanna see the new Grudge on Friday?' I type and hit send. I have to work tomorrow but we should definitely hit the premiere together, I add, and send that, too.

I set my phone on the coffee table in front of me and try to direct my attention back to the TV show, where hosts John and Zack are framing out the bathroom on the bus. Luckily, only two minutes and fourteen seconds pass before my phone dings with an incoming text

B invited us 2 her party Fri. Sry! the text reads, a reply from Crystal.

I exhale a breath I didn't realize I was holding, disappointed. Since when is Bethany one to host a party?

Oh, okay. No worries. Another time! I type back. Have fun, I add as an afterthought, hoping to keep the conversation going. But it doesn't seem to work, because even though the messages show up as delivered, I don't get any further replies from Crystal, and Shelley is silent as ever.

I really want to set things right, but the more I contemplate how to do that, the more I wonder if it's just too late to repair these friendships.

Wednesday, October 13th
Fall of Freshman Year

Like every day since the fight at lunch last week, I'm anxious as I slide into my seat for English class, unsure what today will bring. I can feel the tension radiating off Tyler as he shifts uncomfortably in his chair while I unpack my bag.

"Hey," he practically whispers, giving me a closed-mouth half smile, side-eyeing me as I open my notebook and begin the bell work Mr. Vogel is writing on the board.

"Hey," I reply, giving him my own closed-mouth smile in return. Without much else to say at this point, I go back to my assignment.

While Tyler has kept up the small talk these last few days, the conversation has felt more and more forced the longer Brendan and I aren't speaking. I've been taking my sandwich and hiding out in the library during lunch everyday since then, so I have no idea what the guys have been saying around the lunchroom table. My guess is Tyler doesn't want to get in the middle of it, which I can't say I blame him.

I sneak a glance across the room, not even bother trying to catch Shelley's eye anymore, not after she stuffed earbuds in this morning during study hall, making it glaringly obvious she was over the small talk. Instead, I watch Brendan and Dougie as they chatter on about something. I can't help but wonder if it's me they're talking about.

Whether they can feel my gaze on them or not, neither of them look my way, either simply oblivious to my staring, or actively ignoring me. Between ditching lunch, ditching chess practice, and our mandatory assigned seats in class, I've had minimal contact with Brendan over the last six days, twenty-three hours, two minutes, and twelve seconds. If only he would look over at me, reassure me with the kindness of his eyes or the familiar comfort of his toothy grin, maybe I'd have the courage to apologize.

As I continue burning a hole in the side of Brendan's face, I hear a faint '*ding*' from within the depths of my backpack. When Mr. Vogel's back is turned, I slip my phone out of my bag, unsurprised it's a text from Will.

Who else would it be? Will's about the only one you're on good terms with these days, the annoying part of my brain reminds me.

Every 1 be on time 2day, half hr to prep b4 Merriweather guys show up, his text reads.

I close out of the group thread and open a private message with Will.

Hey, sorry for last minute bail, but I have to work after school today. Won't be at the match.

My fingers move lightning fast and I hit the send button, clicking my phone off and slipping it into my pocket before Mr. Vogel can catch me. It vibrates in my pocket before I can even withdraw my hand, so I slip it back out and peek at it, holding it between my legs in case Mr. Vogel starts walking around the room like he often does during our bell work.

Ditchin again?! Ugh, u suck. U better b there next week or I'm suspending u from next match, Will threatens.

At this point, Mr. Vogel is on the move, but he's at the opposite end of the room, hovering next to Courtney Navid and pointing to something on her paper. I take my chances and punch out a reply.

Please, like you'd ever do that to your MVP, I say, adding a tongue-out emoji to the end of my text.

Tru, he replies. Just get ur shit 2gether n show up next week, k?

Sure thing, boss, I send back, then click my phone off and stow it in my backpack. I glance up and catch Brendan staring across the room at me, but he looks away before I can do anything other than gape back.

So much for trying to catch his eye.

*****

The rest of the school day goes by numbingly slow. I hide out in the library again during lunch, munching on a banana while I read Jurassic Park near the corner windows. Luckily the librarian, Mrs. Wynek, really likes me, so she doesn't bust me for eating in a no-food zone. She leaves me to myself mostly, eyeing me every so often over the counter of the reference desk to make sure I'm okay, but generally giving me my space. I appreciate the silence and solitude the large, empty library affords me, especially considering the alternative was being stuck at an uncomfortable lunch table with a best friend who hates me.

After a boring lecture during History, the final bell rings and releases me from another awkward day of dodging my friends and avoiding my feelings. I slip out the front doors of the school and spot my mom's car. I practically sprint to it, hoping I don't run into anyone outside. Thankfully, I make it to the safety of her car without having to face any of my friends along the way.

"Hi, honey," she greets me cheerfully. "How was school today?"

I groan and click my seatbelt in, slumping down in the seat and staring out the window. "Not every day is butterflies and rainbows, mom," I grumble.

"Well, not with that attitude," she huffs back at me, pressing the car forward through the car loop and back out of the main gates.

As we drive, she goes on about Lauren, updating me on what's new since we saw her last. I'm not really listening, but I interject things like "oh wow," and "really?" and "that's awesome!" nonetheless to make it at least appear like I'm interested in what she's telling me. Finally, what seems like the longest car ride ever ends after an actual twenty-one minutes and six seconds.

"Thanks for the ride, mom," I tell her as she pulls into a parking space in front of the greenhouse.

"Do you need me to pick you up?" she asks.

"No, Carrie said she'll give me a ride home."

"Okay, sweetie. Hope work goes well," she says. "And try to have a little fun!"

"Thanks," I reply with a small smile, and step out of the car.

As my mom pulls out of the parking lot and back onto the main road, I snake my way between the greenhouse and the main storefront, letting myself in a side door that leads directly into the employee break room. I stash my backpack in one of the empty cubbies and grab an apron off the wall peg near the door, tying it around my waist. Then I clock in and push through the door out into the store.

"Janelle!" I hear Carrie cry as I make my way to the cash register. "Thank god you're here," she says when I get closer. "I need to get out to the tree lot and help Reggie with a big order for Sunday, you good for a minute?"

"Of course," I reply. She squeezes my shoulder before hurrying off.

The afternoon goes by in a blur, a welcome distraction from all the drama currently on my plate. You wouldn't think a plant center would be so busy on a random Wednesday in October, but we're the biggest supplier of pumpkins in the area. In fact, it's our biggest seller, second only to Christmas trees.

Finally, after two hours, nine minutes and four seconds, things finally calm down and the pumpkin rush ends. There are a couple customers trickling in here and there, but for the most part, things have died down altogether. Carrie resurfaces, dirt smudged on her cheek and pieces of blonde highlights escaping her hair clip.

"Phew!" she exhales exaggeratedly as she collapses onto the stool behind the counter. She pulls her gloves off and fixes her hair, swooping the strays back up into the clip. Then she pulls a compact mirror from under the counter. "That was madness!" she exclaims, using the mirror to assist in wiping the dirt off her face. "How'd you do in here?" she asks me, looking over at me.

"Great," I tell her. "Madness for sure, but I think we made our sales quota for the day in just those two hours." I laugh when her eyes go wide.

"Nice!" she says, pumping the air with her fist. I resist the urge to dry heave, thinking of one other person I know who pumped the air like that.

"Way to kill it, Nell," she says, drawing me back to the present. She pulls up the sales log on the computer. "Feel free to take a break anytime," she tells me as she scrolls through the log. "You earned it."

"Thanks," I reply. "I just need to use the bathroom and grab a snack, but then I'll head out and start watering the greenhouse."

"You rock," she tells me without looking up from the screen.

I bite my tongue and resist the urge to tell her just how much I *don't* rock, in fact. Instead, I scurry away from the desk back to the employee break room, anxious to get back to doing anything but thinking about my problems.

After a short five-minute-sixteen-second break, I make my way out to the greenhouse. I muster a small wave to the store owner, Reggie, and my coworker, Ethan, as I pass them loading bags of mulch into the back of a customer's pickup.

I enter the greenhouse and unravel the hose in the left corner of the building. I start by watering the plants closest to me, big buckets of ferns and tall grasses that fan out on all sides. I bend down to push away the bushier ones, making sure the water gets directly onto the soil in each tub. When dirt from the pot touches my fingers, I cringe and curse inwardly. I think of the comment I made to Keith about getting dirt under my fingernails, and curse outwardly this time.

After the grasses are thoroughly quenched, I make my way further down the aisle, pulling the hose along behind me. I water the azaleas and rhododendron bushes, trying to keep my thoughts focused on the task, begging my mind to give me just a few moments of peace and quiet where I don't think about anything other than what's right in front of me.

But no matter how hard I try, I can never seem to get that night, and all of its consequences, off my mind. Any quiet, intimate moments with myself are quickly overrun with thoughts of what I've done.

Of all that I've lost.

If it hadn't been for my mistakes, wouldn't Jason and I still be together? Wouldn't Shelley still call me her best friend? There'd be no reason to fight with Brendan, or any of my friends, there'd be nothing keeping me up at night, crying silently until I fall asleep, nothing forcing the sharp edge of metal to my wrist, breaking the skin to release the pain. There'd be none of this agony if I could just go back in time and fix all of this.

To never have done it at all in the first place.

I can feel the blood beneath my skin starting to boil as I weave in and out of the rows of plants, a familiar rage pushing its way past the shield of sadness I've kept up these last few months. I let it bubble up to the surface, feeling a scream building within my chest, and I bite my tongue to keep it in, bellowing in madness within the quiet of my mind instead, screaming the sort of profanities I would never actually have the guts to say out loud.

I'm becoming careless with my watering, splashing the cold liquid haphazardly in, but mostly out of, the giant, decorative pots that hold a cluster of miniature shrubs, not caring anymore. The hard concrete becomes slick beneath my feet and before I can tell myself to calm down, to take a deep breath and get a grip, my foot slips on the wetness.

In a true slow-mo movie moment, I feel myself falling backwards and sideways at the same time, and I put out my arm to try and break my fall. I crash to the concrete floor with a sickening thud, paralyzed for a minute, slumped on my right side in a dazed stupor, before I finally realize what's happened, what I've done.

Panic and shock set in.

This time, I scream for real.

Wednesday, October 13th
Fall of Freshman Year

I'm so groggy when I finally come to that it takes me a minute to realize where I am. As the blurriness in my brain clears, the emergency room sharpens into focus. My mom is sitting in a chair to the left of the bed I'm propped up in, scrolling through her phone; the clock above her head reads 6:38 pm. I've been out for almost forty minutes since they completed the x-rays and MRI scan on my elbow, but it feels like I've only been asleep for five seconds.

"Mom..." I groan, getting her attention. She looks up from her phone.

"Hi sweetie," she says gently. She stands from her chair and comes over to the bed, resting her hand on the bed rail. "How are you feeling?"

"Like I got hit by a bus," I reply, deadpan. "So did I break it?" I ask, my head lolling to the side as I peer down at my arm, wrapped in a beige sling.

"Yes," she nods. "Let me go find the doctor." She slips between the curtains around my bed and scurries off.

While I wait, I try to assess the damage. The first thing I notice as I take stock of my body is that my plain, black, long-sleeved shirt is now one sleeve short. To access my injury, someone (I'm assuming the nurse) cut away the right sleeve of my shirt, but luckily, they left the other side intact, hiding the cuts and scars that crisscross my forearm. If nothing else, at least I won't have to answer any prying questions as to how I got them.

Grateful for this small silver lining, I continue with my assessment. I inhale a deep breath and hold it as I try to slowly wiggle the fingers on my right hand, but I barely move them an inch before pain splits its way through my arm. My face scrunches up in agony and I spit out the breath, a garbled whimper escaping my throat with it. As I contemplate my next move, the curtain rustles and slides to the side, revealing a gap big enough for my mom and the doctor to enter.

My mom resumes her post at the side of my bed while the doctor, a tall, older black man with gray fuzz at his temples, stops at the end of the bed near my feet.

"Hi Janelle," he says, his voice deep and authoritative. "I'm Dr. Sinclair, I'm the orthopedic surgeon here at Marshall General."

"Surgeon?" I ask slowly, confused.

"Yes. You have a very complicated injury," he tells me. He pulls a set of x-rays from the chart that's clipped to the end of the bed and slides them into the portable view box on a rolling stand next to my bed. He flicks it on, illuminating a dislocated joint and a tiny fragmented piece that's split off from the rest of the bone.

"Complicated," I repeat back to him, still woozy from whatever painkillers they gave me when I came in.

Just like me, I think to myself.

The x-ray blurs as I stare at it.

"Yes," he confirms. He points to the x-rays. "You managed to not only break your elbow, but you dislocated the joint and tore all the tendons and ligaments." He pulls the x-ray down and slides the MRI scan into the view box in its place, showing me the tangled mess of soft tissues underneath my skin. It just looks like a blurry gray mass to me, but the serious look on his face tells me it's bad.

"The nurses were able to sedate you and reset the joint when you arrived," he continues, "but unfortunately, we won't be able to repair the remaining damage without surgery."

"What will this mean for recovery?" my mom asks.

"Janelle has a tough road ahead of her," he says, turning towards my mom. "I'm not going to sugarcoat it, I don't believe in that. The surgery should be easy enough, but because of the nature of the injury, we won't be able to put a hard cast on afterwards." He turns back towards me. "You'll need to do daily physical therapy and minimize any further trauma to the area. It will take a lot of time and patience," he continues, "but we should ultimately be able to get you back to your full range of motion prior to the injury."

Should be able to? I panic internally. "So no guarantees I'll be the same?" I ask him, hearing the irony in my words, knowing I haven't been the same since the summer.

"Like I said, as long as you adhere to your physical therapy regimen after the surgery, I see no reason why you won't get full range of motion back. It will just take some time."

I stare at him, unable to form a response.

"So when will she have the surgery?" my mom presses.

"Unfortunately, I'm the only qualified doctor on staff to perform the surgery, and I don't have any openings in my schedule until Sunday," Dr. Sinclair replies.

"I didn't realize scheduling a surgery required you to check your planner first," I grumble, feeling the painkillers wearing off and my annoyance kick in that they aren't just wheeling me off into the operating room as we speak.

"Your injury isn't life-threatening," he says to me. "A few days won't kill you. You will need to keep the sling on until then and be sure not to bump your arm around. You can go to school if you'd like, but you'll need to be excused from classes earlier so you're not in crowded halls where you could get knocked around. I'll write you a note to give to your teachers."

"Can I just stay home?" I ask, perking up at the idea of not having to face my troubles at school for the next two days.

Dr. Sinclair looks at my mom, then back to me. "That's up to you and your family. I'll write you a note for that, too, and you can decide what you prefer. You'll definitely be missing some school after the surgery, so keep that in mind." He pulls an expensive-looking pen from his coat pocket and scribbles something on my chart. "I'll have the nurse get you some Vicodin for any pain you're experiencing now. We'll refill the script once you come back for the surgery. Get some rest over the next few days and I'll see you on Sunday."

He clicks his pen and slides it back into his coat. He clips my chart to the end of the bed, gives me a slight nod and then makes his way back through the curtains, on to his next patient.

After the nurse finishes processing all of my paperwork, and they schedule my surgery for Sunday afternoon, they finally release me. I shuffle out of the ER behind my mom, who is a few steps ahead of me, barking into her phone to fill my dad in on everything the doctor said. We approach the car and she opens the passenger door for me.

"Here," she says, hanging up with my dad and putting her hand out to steady me.

"Thanks," I reply, easing myself into the seat. It takes me a minute to get situated as I fumble with my seatbelt, lifting my arm gently to slide the belt under my elbow and over my lap. When it clicks into place, I collapse back against the seat. My mom clicks the door closed, then scurries around to the driver's side. The car revs to life and we back slowly out of the parking spot before she eases the car out onto the main road.

It becomes instantly obvious that my mom's driving slow for fear of jostling me; her hands are white-knuckled against the steering wheel, as if a firm grip can keep me from feeling any more pain, but even at ten miles below the speed limit, I try not to wince at every bump and turn in the road.

"As soon as we get home, I'll make you something to eat and you can take some pain relief," she says with a quick glance over at me before her eyes dart back to the road. I close my eyes and try not to count every second until we get there.

*****

Between the grilled cheese sandwich my mom made me for dinner and the two tablets of Vicodin I chased it with, I'm feeling pretty good as I lay in bed later that night. After spending the better part of my evening trying to get myself clean in the bathtub (which, come to find out, was basically impossible to do after refusing the help my mom insisted I take), I decided to just crawl into bed and wait for sleep.

I stare up at the ceiling, the faded glow-in-the-dark stick-on constellations that Brendan and I put up years ago twinkling down at me. I rub the fingers of my left hand against my comforter absentmindedly and wonder if it's the shock still or the painkillers that are making me feel so woozy, as if I'm floating.

Or drunk.

With that thought, my mind begins to wander back to that summer night, the only time I've ever actually been drunk before. I feel my head spin with regret as the memory of what I did comes back in flashes.

But just as I feel my heart begin to speed up, panic threatening to overtake my whole body, the heaviness of sleep finds me.

I close my eyes and let the night consume me.

Saturday, October 16th
Fall of Freshman Year

"Janelle, Brendan is on the phone again," my mom says Saturday afternoon, thrusting the landline towards me where I'm sprawled on the couch, her hand covering the speaker slats in the receiver.

"No thanks," I mumble, my eyes glued to the TV, unmoving except for my mouth.

She gives me a look and sighs before walking away.

"She's resting right now, hon," I hear her tell him before I let my mind drift away again, the Vicodin I took thirty minutes earlier taking over.

When my eyes flutter open again, my mom is sitting in the recliner next to the couch, an episode of Oprah on the TV. I draw in a deep breath and groan, trying to swallow back the grogginess that's set in now that the Vicodin has worn off. At the sound of me stirring, my mom looks over at me.

"Hi honey," she says, standing up and switching off the TV. "How are you feeling? Can I get you anything?"

"Water, please," I croak.

"Sure."

She pads out of the living room and into the kitchen. I hear her clinking around in the cabinet for a glass, then the sound of the ice machine as she fills the glass with crushed ice. I reach my left arm out towards the coffee table, inching my phone over towards my fingers until it's close enough to grab.

One glance at the home screen reminds me that I still have four missed calls and eight unread texts from Brendan, nineteen unread texts in the group thread with Brendan, Dougie, and Tyler, two unread texts from Crystal and one unread text from Shelley. I sigh, still unable to bring myself to read any of them, even days later. I set my phone back down on the table as my mom comes in with a glass of ice water and a package of saltines.

"Thought you might want to try and eat something," she says as she sets the crackers and glass on the table within reach. She notices the messages on my phone.

"Sweetheart, you really shouldn't keep avoiding your friends like that," she says. "They're all worried about you and want to make sure you're okay. Brendan has been calling for days, you really should get back to him."

"Yeah, okay," I tell her, nodding slightly.

"I have some paperwork to do, but just holler if you need anything."

She leaves me to my snack, wandering back through the kitchen to the home office at the far end of the house, where she works most days helping my dad run his roofing company.

I push a saltine into my mouth, holding it on my tongue and sucking all the salt out of it until it turns to mush. I chew the mush and swallow it, tipping the glass of water slightly towards my face and sipping the cold liquid slowly. It settles my stomach a bit so I eat another cracker and follow it with another small sip of water.

Feeling a bit more alert now, I think about what my mom said, and she's right, though not in the way she meant it. If I keep dodging everyone, what's to stop them from just showing up at my house unexpectedly? I can't have any of them see me like this, so I decide to finally just tackle the messages on my phone before my panicked heart has the chance to burst its way out of my chest. I open the thread between the guys first, scrolling back up to where they started two days, four hours, six minutes and eight seconds ago.

Brendan: Hey, where u at? Shelley said u weren't in 1st period

Dougie: Just the fact that we had 2 resort 2 asking Shelley where u are is making me concerned, so u better tell us what's up

Tyler: Yeah, what's with the radio silence, Nell? Not like u

Brendan: Just let us know u haven't been abducted by aliens or something

Dougie: Well if she was abducted by aliens, I doubt they would give her access to a phone to let us know that she was abducted by aliens

Brendan: Dude, shut up. No one asked u

Dougie: I mean, u kinda did...

Brendan: Nell, if u don't answer, we're going to assume ur incapacitated in 1 way or another & we'll have no choice but to storm the gates & come to ur rescue

I can't help but smile at the back and forth between the guys as they describe the various scenarios that I may have gotten caught up in, and the different rescue methods they've concocted to relieve me of my imprisonment. If only the truth was actually that exciting and less pathetic.

I scroll to the bottom of the thread, where it appears Brendan must have told the others what happened (no doubt prying it out of my mom while I was hopped up on painkillers), because they each send their individual well wishes, asking me to keep them posted and let them know if they can do anything. Dougie offers to get my assignments for me, and Tyler promises not to let Mr. Vogel reassign my seat to anyone in class.

I break my silence by sending a quick text to them.

I'm hanging in, thanks. I add a heart emoji and hit send. No sooner is it delivered than a reply from Dougie comes back.

SHE LIVES!

I smile and close out of the text. Since the guys' thread was easier than I expected, I keep the momentum going and move on to Crystal's private messages.

Hey, everythng OK? Missed u in class 2day

Heard about ur arm, so sry! Let me kno if there's anything I can do

Although the gesture is sweet, that's all she's said since Thursday afternoon. It's hard to feel comforted by an offer to help when she can't even be bothered to check in on me again. I swipe out of Crystal's message without replying and open Shelley's, although one measly text can't hold all that much, so I'm not holding my breath.

Sure enough, her text, which is time stamped much later in the afternoon on Thursday than all the others, contains only eleven words and two punctuation marks.

Sorry 2 hear about ur arm, hope u get well soon

Her message reads like a poorly-written Hallmark card.

I'm not even sure I care anymore.

I swipe left to delete the message. Then I open Brendan's private texts, nervous that he'll be angrier here than he was in the group thread.

Hey, where are u? U okay?

What's going on? No one can reach u

Nell, let me know what's up. Are u good, or what?

Seriously, please reply & at least let me know ur alive

Don't make me get in my mom's car & drive over there on my learner's permit Cause u know I'll do it

Nell, wtf, I know ur mad at me but c'mon, this is stupid. Answer me

Ur mom told me what happened, shit. Call me back

Nell, please call me. I need to know ur okay

I reread his messages one more time, relief spreading through me as I realize he's not still harboring a secret hatred towards me. I swallow my fear and hit the call button next to his name. It only rings once before he picks up.

"Hey, how are you? I'm so glad you called finally." His voice is even but I can hear the relief in his words.

"Hey," I breathe, "I'm doing okay, for now. Just tired and achy. Surgery isn't until tomorrow. I guess I just feel like an idiot for falling and breaking a bone. Didn't think I was that much of a klutz," I tell him, trying to laugh at my predicament.

"Happens to the best of us, am I right?" Brendan replies, referring to the time he tripped over a tree stump and broke his toe. Although not quite the same type of injury, I appreciate his attempt at solidarity.

"I guess so," I say, nodding even though he can't see me. I clear my throat, anxious to get past the elephant in the room. "Look, about the other day..."

"I get it," he interjects. "You were mad in the heat of the moment. I'm just sorry for being such an ass and saying what I did. You didn't deserve that." He pauses. "Anyone should be so lucky to be your boyfriend," he adds.

I'm grateful that he can't see me blush at his kind words, even though his original point was valid. I *don't* have a boyfriend, with good reason. And why would anyone *want* to be my boyfriend at this point? Considering how I treated the last one, I don't deserve to be anyone's girlfriend. I almost say the words out loud, but I can't stand the idea of him knowing what I did, so I settle on an apology instead.

"I'm sorry, too. My temper just got away from me. You were only trying to help. I appreciate that," I tell him. "I guess I just let everything with Jason get under my skin."

"No worries," he tells me. "Just keep fightin' the good fight. Forget about those haters and you'll get through. And don't ever ignore me again," he adds. "I can't stand the thought that something's going on with you and I can't do anything about it. Least you can do is give me a heads-up, y'know?"

I *do* know, and that thought gets to me, goosebumps breaking out all over my body. I silently tell myself to calm down, that Brendan's only referring to my injury, and maybe even the fight with Jason. There's no possible way he knows what I did to cause all of this to spiral so out of control. Only two people actually know what I did that night, and the only person besides me who could tell my secret lives 478 miles south of here. And to him, I probably don't even exist anymore.

I swallow back the lump building in my throat, pushing it down along with the memories of that night. As long as I can stay composed, Brendan doesn't have to suspect anything.

"Okay," I finally answer. "Thanks."

"Let me know how the surgery goes, okay?" he replies.

"I will."

Feeling a bit braver once I hang up with Brendan, I open Instagram. I know it's only been three days, two hours, twenty-six minutes and eight seconds since I was last at school, but I already feel out of the loop.

I scroll past a photo Dougie posted this morning, he and Will locked in a match from chess practice Wednesday. I hit the "like" button, then leave a comment.

Did Will actually win this one?? I write, adding a wink emoji and hitting *post*.

I keep scrolling past the random announcements from the verified accounts I follow, *'liking'* a photo from Netflix about an upcoming show they're filming and leaving a heart emoji on a picture of Thailand from one of the travel bloggers I follow.

But as I scroll further back in my feed, I come up on a post from Crystal, time stamped yesterday at 10:22 pm. The photo is clearly from Bethany's party; Crystal, Shelley, and Bethany are all smiling at the camera, and I can see several people in the background, clearly enjoying themselves as the party rages on around them.

Gr8 times w/ gr8 friends! Crystal's caption reads.

Best party 4 sure! Shelley had commented.

My stomach sinks. A year ago, I would have been in that picture with the three of them. Instead, I've been stuck at home, nursing a broken arm, while they're off having the time of their lives, clearly not even missing me one little bit.

I sigh and scroll past the photo without *'liking'* or commenting. But no sooner do I swipe up and away from the picture of the three of them than a picture of Bethany and Jason pops up in its place. I can feel my heart rate increasing as I stare at the screen.

Love u baby! Best girlfriend ever, Jason's caption reads.

My breath catches in my throat. After what I did to him, I know I deserve this. I wasn't a good girlfriend; in fact, I was probably the worst girlfriend there ever was, even if he doesn't actually know why. But his words only serve as a blatant reminder to everyone else that, compared to Bethany, I'm completely inadequate. My stomach tightens and twists into anxious knots as I keep reading the comments.

My ride or die! Bethany had replied, followed by a bunch of heart emojis. Twelve people "liked" her comment.

Even though I still haven't overcome the feeling of betrayal I have towards Bethany, I find myself relating to her, even in this painful moment. For a time, Jason was *my* ride or die. As a form of torture, I keep reading what others have written.

Perfect couple! Shelley had said.

Love u 2! So cute! Crystal had commented.

As frustrating as it is to see Shelley and Crystal supporting Bethany's relationship with Jason, their comments are mild compared to some of the others.

Beth's a babe, def way better than that troll u were w/ dude! someone I don't know had said.

True love! another person had written.

And you don't have to worry about Bethany ditching you for no reason LOL someone else had replied.

I slam my phone down on the couch next to me, not wanting to read any more. Hot, angry tears burn their way out of my eyes and down my cheeks. I want to scream at everyone, to tell them there *was* a reason I went AWOL and broke it off with Jason. I just don't know which would be worse: everyone *thinking* I'm a heartless bitch for dumping him without an explanation, or knowing for *sure* that I'm a heartless bitch for what I actually did to him.

I feel the heartache I had pushed deep within me surfacing, making the throbbing in my elbow feel like a piece of cake. While my fingers itch for a sharp object, I grab the bottle of Vicodin off the coffee table instead and pop one in my mouth, crumpling back into the couch as I wait for it to carry me away from my pain.

Sunday, October 17th
Fall of Freshman Year

When my parents and I pull into the hospital parking lot at 12:19 pm the next day, I'm surprisingly calm. Though I slipped myself an extra Vicodin this morning with breakfast, I can tell the effects of the painkiller have worn off, which means the peace I'm feeling is all me. I think my brain has finally realized that Dr. Sinclair is about to take care of this whole elbow mess, and the agony I've experienced the last few days will soon be over.

At least I can get one nightmare off my plate.

My dad drops my mom and me at the curb before heading off in search of a parking space. We enter the hospital's main entrance, check in at the front desk and find a seat in the main waiting room. Unlike the ER, we don't wait long, heading back to the operating room just eight minutes and eleven seconds after arriving.

They bring me back in a wheelchair, which feels unnecessary, considering I walked myself into the building, but I lean back in the chair and take advantage of the extra comfort.

"We'll be right here when you wake up, sweetheart," my dad assures me as he and my mom split off at the doors to the OR.

"Okay." My voice shakes a little and my smile wavers as I realize they aren't coming with me. They smile back at me, my mom giving me a small wave of encouragement as I'm wheeled through the double doors and out of their sight.

The nurses help me change out of my clothes and into a hospital gown. As I slide my left arm into the gown quickly, I'm thankful for the makeup I applied this morning, covering my scars from prying eyes, warding off any unwanted questions. I'm embarrassed to think of how careless I've been, so cliched and obvious, as if I were dying for attention. The idea of a spotlight shining on me sends a shiver up my spine, but then I remember the bottle of Vicodin and its never-ending refills waiting for me when I get home, and I can feel myself relaxing a bit.

I finish dressing and the nurses help me get situated on the operating table as Dr. Sinclair enters.

"Hello, Janelle," he says, pulling on a pair of gloves. "How are you feeling?"

"Pretty crummy," I tell him honestly. "Ready for this to just be over."

He chuckles. "Well, I'll certainly see what I can do about that. Shouldn't be more than a few hours and we'll have you all fixed up."

They strap a mask over my face and I feel a gentle flow of something seeping into my mouth and nose.

"If you could slowly count backwards from ten, please," one of the nurses tells me.

"Ten...nine...eight...seven..."

I fade away into nothingness.

*****

When I come to hours later, it takes me a minute to remember where I am, but the ache in my arm as I shift in the hospital bed quickly reminds me. I groan as I wipe away the sleep in my eyes.

"Hi, honey," I hear my mom whisper from across the room.

"Hey, sleepyhead," my dad chimes in.

They both rise from the chairs they're sitting in, coming over to my bed.

"How are you feeling?" my mom asks.

"Like hell," I respond, forgetting to censor my language in front of them, but they just chuckle. "How'd it go?" I ask.

"Good," my dad replies. "Doc was able to reattach all your torn tendons and ligaments, and fused the broken bit back in place. He even added some super hi-tech robot muscle so you can fight crime with ease." He grins goofily down at me.

I try to laugh at his ridiculous dad joke but it comes out as more of a wheeze instead. My whole body trembles with the effort, shooting pain up my newly-repaired arm. I try to cover my wince, but my mom sees it anyway.

"Take it easy, Nell," she reminds me, smoothing my hair. "Just try and rest."

"How long will we be here?" I want to know.

"The doctor said as soon as the morphine wears off, we can go. We'll have to come back in a week for a follow-up, but we've already got your Vicodin refill and the removable brace for the days in between." She gestures at a robotic-looking brace on the table in the corner of the room.

"You're gonna be unstoppable in that thing," my dad says encouragingly, giving me two thumbs up. At least he has enough enthusiasm for the both of us.

Over the next three hours, nine minutes, and forty-one seconds, I laze about in the hospital bed, rotating between watching the TV, listening to my dad's horrible jokes, and dozing off.

Finally, the nurse clears me to go, so I change out of the hospital gown into a pair of sweats and a baggy t-shirt my mom brought from home. I try to silence the panic building in me, longing for the safety of my wristbands as the blemished skin of my left arm becomes exposed once I pull on the shirt, the makeup having started to cake and wear off. I settle into the wheelchair the nurse has provided, cradling my right arm with my left, hoping everyone will be too focused on the one to notice the other.

I endure another wheelchair ride back down to the parking lot, grateful once we pull up next to the car. I slowly ease my way into the back seat, holding onto my mom for support. When I'm finally in, I slump against the door and try to get comfortable.

Unlike the ride home from the hospital the first time, where every bump and turn in the road made me want to scream, I've got such a high dose of painkillers in me this time that I hardly notice the drive at all. We're pulling into the driveway before

I've even had a chance to count the minutes since we left the hospital.

"I'm going to make you some soup, okay, honey?" my mom says as we enter the kitchen off the garage, my dad helping me toward the stairs. "I'll bring it up when it's ready. Here, take this with you, Darrell," she tells my dad, passing him a bottle of water from the fridge, and my bottle of Vicodin.

"Thanks, mom," I reply.

I hobble up the stairs, leaning against my dad to avoid falling. We shuffle into my bedroom, where he helps me ease into bed. He props the pillows up behind me so I can rest at an angle, alleviating some of the weight on my arm. He sets the bottle of water and pills on my nightstand, within reach of my good arm.

"Need anything else, sweetie?" he asks, hovering next to me.

"I'm good," I tell him. He leans down and kisses my forehead before turning to leave. He pulls my bedroom door behind him, leaving it ajar, before clomping his way down the stairs.

After a minute, I hear the muffled voices of my parents in the kitchen downstairs, directly under my bedroom. I grab for the bottle of water and the Vicodin, shaking two pills into my hand and swallowing them down with a large gulp of water. Unable to screw the caps back on, I simply set them off to the side of my nightstand, and lean back into my pillows.

I close my eyes to rest, thinking about the steaming hot bowl of chicken noodle that's headed my way, but without meaning to, I fall asleep instead.

Thursday, October 21st
Fall of Freshman Year

I'm scrolling through the camera roll on my phone, debating whether I should finally delete the pictures of Jason and me I still have stored there, when there's a knock on the front door.

"It's open!" I yell loudly from the living room.

I swipe out of the photos and click my phone off, setting it down on the coffee table next to a half empty bottle of Vitaminwater. I grab the wrappers and tissues that litter the table, stuffing them into an empty Doritos bag as I hear the front door open. I smooth my pin-straight hair behind my ears as the door closes again.

"Nell?" Brendan calls out from around the corner. I hear a shuffle of feet as he and Dougie kick their shoes off, both of them sticklers for my parents' house rules, even though I tell them every time they come over not to worry about it.

"In here," I reply.

"Hey," Brendan says as he pokes his head around the corner from the hallway. He makes eye contact with me before stepping down into the sunken living room, Dougie at his heels.

I smile as I take them both in, having missed the sight of them. Brendan's got a black beanie pulled over his fiery hair, hands shoved deep in the pockets of his jeans and a "What Would Frodo Do?" shirt pulled tight across his broad chest.

Dougie's brown eyes are visible for once without the thick, black glasses he usually wears obscuring them from view. His green "Loch Chess Monster" shirt pops against his dark pants as he plops onto the leather La Z Boy across the room.

"So how you feelin'?" Brendan asks as he slumps down onto the suede couch next to me. "All things considered," he adds. He crosses his left ankle over his right, hands clasped behind his head, and leans back into the couch.

"Oh, y'know, the usual. Excruciating pain radiating out from my elbow at any given moment, dizzy spells when I get up after laying down too long, unable to shower on my own. That sort of thing." I answer sarcastically, waving his question away with my left hand.

"Well, you look great!" Brendan replies playfully, giving my arm an air punch.

"Yeah, love the new look, Nell," Dougie chimes in, smiling as he gestures towards the robotic-looking elbow brace on my elbow.

"You could give Iron Man a run for his money," Brendan says.

"Or RoboCop," Dougie counters.

"You guys," I reply, rolling my eyes.

"No, no, I see it," Brendan continues, waving me away. "RoboNell."

"3000," Dougie adds.

"Yes! That's it! RoboNell 3000, half girl, half machine. Full badass," Brendan says, gesturing with his hands as if pitching a movie.

"I think you messed up the tagline," Dougie corrects him.

"Who cares? It's still awesome," Brendan goes on. "Here, Nell," he says, pulling out his phone. "Strike a pose."

He snaps a photo before I can protest, smiling in satisfaction as he types something out on the screen of his phone.

"Hey, don't post that…" I start. It's one thing for these guys to see me like this, but the last thing I want is for anyone *else* to see me this way.

"Don't worry, Nell, you look way cool," Brendan says, ignoring my request and sliding his phone back into his pocket.

I bite my lower lip, trying not to make a big deal of it.

"So when will you be back at school?" Dougie asks, back to business. "Chess sucks without you."

"*Everything* sucks without you," Brendan adds, staring at me.

"Thanks, guys," I say, struggling to maintain eye contact. "I'm not sure when I'll be back. Hopefully within a week or two. I have a follow-up with the doctor on Sunday, so he'll let me know what's up."

"Okay, cool, just keep us in the loop," Dougie says. "Obviously we want you to rest and get better. But man, do we need you back on the team bad."

"Plus, we just want you back at school with us," Brendan goes on. "Shit hasn't been the same without you there."

"Oh my god, tell her what happened in English yesterday," Dougie says, excitedly, his brown eyes going wide.

"Oh right," Brendan remembers. "Nell, you're gonna laugh your ass off at this."

"What? What happened?" I ask, genuinely curious.

"So Vogel had us doing a role play for Animal Farm," he starts.

"And ironically Shelley volunteered for the role of Napoleon," Dougie adds.

"Right," Brendan goes on, standing up from the couch in his excitement, "so she's trying her best to get all into her character-"

"Which isn't hard, considering how loud and bossy Napoleon is," Dougie interjects.

"Can I tell the story?" Brendan asks, turning to him. Dougie gives him a look but gestures for him to proceed. "So she's up at the front of the class, belting out her lines," he goes on, swiveling his hips and flicking his head back and forth in what I assume is a Shelley imitation, "When she belts out the nastiest burp instead."

"It was so gross and awesome," Dougie practically shouts.

"Her face turned beet red. She tried to laugh it off with the rest of us, but you could tell she was embarrassed, even after everyone quieted down and continued with the role play. It was priceless." Brendan flops back down onto the couch next to me, satisfaction oozing out of him.

"Wow," is all I can say, wincing in embarrassment on Shelley's behalf. If it had been any of the guys that had happened to, I'm sure they would've been reenacting it for days, doubled over in laughter at how hysterical it was, zero embarrassment felt by any. But knowing Shelley, she must have been completely mortified. In fact, she probably still is. I can't help but feel sorry for her, even after the lack of empathy on her part lately.

I try to put it out of my mind as Dougie changes the topic, going on about the match against Jefferson tomorrow that I'm going to miss. They tell me about other random things that have happened since I've been out, like the juniors that got caught smoking weed in the auditorium and the new substitute science teacher all the girls have been fawning over. Brendan tells me his thoughts on the newest Stranger Things episode, and Dougie gives me his thoughts on running for class president next year.

Before I know it, forty-six minutes and eight seconds have passed since they arrived. I can feel the most recent Vicodin I took wearing off. My fingers twitch, eager to reach out and grab the bottle. I stifle an exaggerated yawn, which they both notice, moving to get up.

"We should get outta your hair," Brendan says, adjusting his jeans as he stands.

"Oh hey, before I forget…" Dougie trails off, disappearing into the front hallway. He comes back with a stack of papers and books, passing them to me. "I got your work from last week and this week. I didn't know how long you'd be out, so I figured this was a good start," he explains, crossing his arms over his chest.

"Thanks," I reply, setting the assignments on the coffee table. "I should be back within a week or two, but this will keep me busy for awhile. "

"No worries," he says. "Let us know if you need anything else, and when you're taking visitors again." He gives me a big, goofy grin.

"Yeah, I'm glad you changed your mind about having us over. It was really good to see you, Nell," Brendan adds.

"Likewise," I nod.

They see themselves out and I settle back into the couch, grabbing for my phone again. I open a new text to Shelley, debating what to say. If I had been humiliated like that in front of my classmates, I know I'd want her to reach out. But what to say?

The more I think about it, the more I realize I don't really even know her that much anymore. Hearing about her embarrassing moment in English from the guys instead of from her just reminds me that Shelley hasn't told me much of anything since the summer. Before all of this started. She's been confiding in others, people like Crystal and Bethany, and her new boyfriend and all their band friends, not me. I've just been getting the run-off through the grapevine.

From what I've seen since school started, she's definitely not the same Shelley who bought me tampons for the first time in seventh grade, barging right up to the cashier without any hesitation when I was too nervous to do it myself. And I doubt these days she would come over and devour a whole pint of Ben & Jerry's with me while I cried over my elbow, over Jason, over all of it.

But then again, I haven't told her much of anything since August, either, so I guess I can't be too shocked that she's pulled away. Would I feel the same if the tables were turned? Because I'm not the same Janelle who used to tell her best friend every secret, even the messy ones that hurt to say out loud. So I guess when you look at it this way, I don't deserve to be her friend anymore.

After a moment's hesitation, I put my phone back down on the table without texting her. Instead, I pop two Vicodin and lay down on my side, closing my eyes while I wait for the numbness to kick in.

Friday, October 22nd
Fall of Freshman Year

I'm laying on the couch in a haze, watching reruns of Siesta Key, when my phone buzzes from deep within the cushions. I wiggle onto my side and dig around for a minute before my fingers close over my battered iPhone, pulling it free.

My eyes go wide when I see a text from Keith on the screen.

Hey, how's it going? Heard about your arm, that really sucks. Here if you want to talk, it says.

Stunned, it takes me a minute to process. Finally, after fumbling with my left hand as I punch in my passcode, I get my messages open. The text glares up at me, waiting for a reply, but I'm unsure how to respond. After our last encounter, I know Keith is just reaching out to be polite, but it's unnerving all the same. Thankfully, the drugs in my system, in addition to relieving any pain in my elbow, do a good job suppressing my anxiety, and without being fully aware of what I'm doing, I find myself typing out a reply and hitting send before my brain can tell my body not to.

I'm hanging in there, I reply. It definitely sucks, but I guess it could be worse, right? I add.

What do you have to be so optimistic about? my brain taunts me.

Glad to hear. Saw a picture of you on Insta and, while you looked as cute as ever, that thing you have to wear does **not** look like fun. Can't imagine what hell you're living in right now.

He follows his text with a tongue-out smiley emoji, trying to lighten the mood.

I'm about to text back 'what picture?' but then it hits me; that god-awful picture Brendan took of me yesterday is still floating around the internet somewhere.

Goddamnit, Brendan.

I swipe out of my texts and open Instagram, going directly to Brendan's profile. There it is, second photo in, grinning horribly back up at me, with thirty-one likes, twenty-four comments, and who knows how many shares.

I quickly scan the comments, which seem to be a mixture of well-wishes and insults, from friends, acquaintances and enemies alike. Not surprising, since Brendan's account is public. For every sympathetic *"hope you get well soon, Janelle!"* there seems to be a nasty comment tearing me down and making fun of me for a plethora of reasons. Unsurprisingly, there's one from Keith's ex, Megan, reminding everyone what a freak I am, followed by several replies from her cheerleading posse agreeing with her in various ways. Among the rude remarks, there are many encouraging ones from my chess teammates, wanting to know when the star player will be back on the team, and there are even several comments questioning why I don't have a regular cast which, while harmless in nature, all serve as reminders of what a shitty hand I've been dealt.

Payback for all the shit you've put everyone else through, right? I think.

Having forgotten about Keith in my frustration, I swipe back to my messages and instead open the thread between Brendan and me.

I shouldn't have let you come over yesterday, I stab at the screen. I didn't want anyone to see me like this! WTF BRENDAN?! TAKE THAT PHOTO DOWN!!!

Without waiting for a reply, I turn my phone on silent and throw it across the room, where it bounces off the wall and tumbles to the floor, out of reach.

Fuming, I swipe my bottle of pills off the table and shake two into my hand. I hesitate for a minute before dumping a third pill onto my palm, slapping them to my mouth and swallowing them down with a warm sip of day-old juice. I throw myself back against the couch, breathing heavily out of my nostrils, and wait for the pills to kick in and my anger to melt away.

*****

I wake later, groggy and unsure what time it is, an overwhelming urge to pee distracting me from anything else. After dragging myself to the downstairs bathroom off the kitchen, I stumble my way back to the living room. I begrudgingly grab my phone off the floor and bring it with me to the couch, where I all but collapse back down into the Janelle-shaped indent in the cushions.

As the fogginess from the painkillers and extra-long nap I took slowly fades, I remember my anger from earlier. I open my texts, ignoring the last message from Keith that I still have yet to answer and going right to the string of messages Brendan's sent since.

Shit, Nell, I'm sorry, I didn't think it would be such a big deal. I'll take it down right now

Okay, it's deleted. I'm really sorry. I didn't mean to upset u

Janelle? C'mon, don't shut me out again. Plz. I'm sorry

I reread the angry text I sent, my cheeks turning red with embarrassment and my insides doing somersaults of shame at losing my temper on him again. I'm not entirely sure at what point along the way I became so short-fused, but I think I have a pretty good guess. I just know I've already lost so many other friends, I can't afford to lose him, too, so I swallow my unease and type out an apology.

No, I'm the one who should be sorry. I lost it over nothing. I just want to get back to normal so badly, and it seems like no matter what I do, that just won't happen.

I hit send, waiting for the message to show as delivered, and then read. My heart rate picks up as I stare down at the screen, watching the three little dots appear, then disappear, then reappear as he types out a reply.

It'll be ok, he says. Pretty soon u will be all healed up, & this will all be behind u. He follows his text with a heart emoji, but it does little to lift my spirits.

Because I know, deep down, that he's wrong. This isn't about a broken elbow; I'd *be* so lucky if that was my only problem. No, this is much bigger than an accidental injury.

I'm just starting to worry how much more I can handle, with each new problem chipping away at what's left of me, before I break apart entirely.

Sunday, October 24th
Fall of Freshman Year

"Sweetie, we have to leave in about half an hour," my mom calls to me from the kitchen, where she's making us sandwiches.

"Twenty-six minutes and eleven seconds," I mumble under my breath from my spot on the couch. As I wait for my lunch, bare feet tapping against the coffee table, I continue trolling TikTok, trying to find entertaining videos from random strangers and avoiding my friends' accounts at all costs. Although, I don't even know why I'm still calling some of them friends, considering Shelley and Crystal haven't reached out in any way since I first broke my arm.

Good luck 2day, a text from Brendan interrupts me, blinking at the top of my phone to remind me that there are still *some* friends who care about me. Let me know how it goes, another one pops up in its place, lingering for a minute before disappearing again.

I sigh and close out of the video app, opening my texts, where Brendan's message sits front and center waiting to be read. I ignore the text from Keith that I still haven't answered, wondering if I should just delete it since I'm not planning on replying to it anytime soon. Or ever.

Thanks, I will, I write back to Brendan.

I set my phone down, my mind suddenly distracted from senseless social media, instead becoming more anxious the closer my follow-up appointment with Dr. Sinclair gets. I know there's no validation to my worry; there's no logical reason for me to think something will ultimately go wrong today, but I can't seem to quelch the unease roiling in my gut nonetheless. I try to distract myself by picking at the lint on my sweatpants.

"Here you go, Nell," my mom says as she enters the living room, passing me a plate of food. She's made me ham and cheese on a toasted everything bagel with a pickle on the side. But despite the rumbling in my stomach, I can't do much more than nibble at it.

"You feeling okay?" she asks as she eats her own sandwich, perched daintily on the edge of the

La-Z-Boy across the room. She dabs at the corners of her mouth with the edge of a napkin.

"Yeah, just not very hungry, I guess," I lie, breaking off bits of the bagel and making a tiny mountain on my plate out of them.

"Well, I'll wrap it up and you can take it to go in case you get hungry on the way to the doctor's."

I try to force a little more, knowing my weak body needs the fuel. I take a bite of the pickle, but the juice is extra sour on my tongue, making my eyes water. I set the plate back on the coffee table and nudge it slightly away from me, trying not to act ungrateful. Luckily, my mom doesn't say anything more, just comes over to collect it, giving me a quick kiss on the head before making her way back into the kitchen. I hear her digging around in a drawer for a sandwich bag before making her way back to the living room.

"Few more minutes and we'll go, okay?" she reminds me as she passes through on her way upstairs.

"Okay," I answer.

I drag myself off the couch and follow her, trudging slowly up the stairs and into the bathroom I no longer have to share with my sister, closing the door behind me with a gentle *click*. I use the toilet, washing my left hand the best I can without the other one to assist. I run a brush through my tangled, unwashed hair, longing to pull it back into a ponytail. I stare at my haggard reflection in the mirror, wishing I could change out of the blue, oversized t-shirt I'm wearing, but I know there's no real point. Instead, I adjust the wristbands on my left wrist and tighten the drawstring on my grey sweatpants.

I slip out of the bathroom and head back downstairs, grabbing my phone from the living room and shuffling my way to the front door. I stuff my feet into a pair of slide-on Vans before letting myself out.

When I get to the driveway, my mom is down by the horse paddock, throwing bales of hay over the fence for Lucy and Rambo. I kick at the blacktop while I wait for her, ignoring the scuffs it makes on my white shoes. I fight the urge to run back inside and hide under the covers, knowing no matter where I go, my problems will follow.

"Ready?" my mom asks as she saunters up the sloped yard towards the car.

"Sure," I say, not really sure at all.

We climb into the car and fasten our seatbelts. My mom turns the key and the engine hums to life. I fiddle with the radio dial as she backs out of our driveway.

"How you feelin'?" she asks once we're out on the main road, glancing over at me where I'm slumped over the center console.

"Nervous," I admit, sucking my teeth as I stare out the windshield.

"It's okay to be nervous, Nell," she tells me. "But don't overly worry yourself. I'm sure everything will be fine."

"Will it?" I blurt out, turning to face her. She makes a face and sighs.

"Of course, sweetheart. Why wouldn't it be?"

I ignore what I assume is a rhetorical question anyway and go back to staring out the window. But my mom doesn't give up that easily, and she tries to reel me back into the conversation again.

"If you're worried about Florida, we'll just have to wait and see what Dr. Sinclair says. We can always go another time."

I scrunch my eyebrows together and sigh, wishing she understood.

"Whatever," I grumble.

I turn the radio up louder and hope she gets the hint.

Sunday, October 24th
Fall of Freshman Year

After another fourteen minutes and thirty-nine seconds driving in silence, we finally pull up to the hospital's outpatient building. Instead of dropping me at the door like my dad did last time, my mom slides into a parking spot right away, forcing me to walk with her through the visitor's lot on our way to the main entrance. At this point, though, she doesn't try to make small talk with me.

We enter through the sliding doors and my mom makes her way to the reception desk. I take the opportunity to slump into the nearest chair.

"Janelle Beckley for Dr. Sinclair," I hear her tell the nurse at the front desk. They exchange pleasantries while the nurse signs me in.

I look around the waiting room, wondering what brings everyone else to this miserable place. I lock eyes with a little boy, maybe six or seven years old, with wispy blonde hair and a Hulk t-shirt. I crack a half smile at him but he just buries his face in his mom's side.

"They'll be out for us momentarily," my mom tells me as she sits down in the chair next to me. She grabs a copy of Home & Garden and a copy of the Oprah Magazine off the glass coffee table in front of us. She holds out the Home & Garden to me, a jack-o-lantern plastered on the cover, and I reluctantly take it from her.

I stare down at the smiling pumpkin with its lopsided grin, and my eyes glaze over, thinking about all the pumpkins I sold at work the last time I was there, when I broke my elbow, leading me here.

I shouldn't have even been at work in the first place, I think.

In fact, if it wasn't for that fight with Brendan at lunch, I wouldn't have needed an excuse to skip chess practice, and I would have just told Carrie I couldn't cover the shift. My angry thoughts pull me deeper into the rabbit hole, bouncing from the fight with Brendan to the fight with Jason, back further in time to our breakup, and the real reason everything has turned to shit since the summer. As I continue to stare unblinkingly down at the magazine cover, the toothy jack-o-lantern's face begins to morph into *his*.

It's the first time since that night that I've let his face worm its way back into my thoughts, the wall I've built in my mind starting to crack, letting those details I never wanted to remember start to slip through. I can hear the magazine crinkling between my fingers as my grip on it tightens, my eyes still glued to the pumpkin-turned-surfer-boy, his sparkling teeth smiling back up at me, his blue eyes twinkling, sun-bleached hair flopping seductively over his forehead. Seeing his face in my mind, my blood starts to boil beneath my skin, and I feel a slew of curse words wet on my tongue, ready to explode out of me.

"Janelle?" my mom's voice interjects.

"What?" I say, dazed. I blink a few times and the pumpkin is just a pumpkin again. I release my death grip, smoothing the dented cover back out and setting the magazine back on the pile on the table.

"I asked if you were ready? They called us back." My mom gestures to a nurse hovering nearby, smiling softly, trying to hide the impatience on her face.

"Oh," I reply. "Yeah, okay."

After a round of x-rays and an MRI, the nurse leads me back down a series of hallways, navigating the twists and turns in the building with ease. I watch her blonde ponytail swish with each step and wonder how long she's worked here, if she likes her job. I try to imagine how many patients she's had to give bad news to, how she keeps her composure during the really upsetting moments.

My musings are interrupted as she stops abruptly in front of an open door, directing me into a sterile-looking patient room, where my mom is already seated in a chair against one wall.

"How'd it go?" my mom asks as we enter.

"Good, I guess?" I reply.

"The doctor will be in shortly to review the scans with you both," the nurse tells my mom. "Have a seat on the table," she turns and says to me, gesturing towards the metal table in the middle of the room.

I awkwardly hop up, scooting until the backs of my knees are flush against the edge. My mom watches my movements, crossing her right leg over her left and pushing her hair away from her face.

We both sit silently as the nurse busies herself with taking my blood pressure and heart rate. She scribbles a few things on my chart as I stifle a yawn.

"I'll be right back with Dr. Sinclair," she tells me, and floats out of the room, closing the door behind her.

After the nurse leaves, I look down at my elbow for the first time since the surgery. With the bandages removed, I can see what a mess it truly is. The entire joint is slightly swollen, a mixture of purple, black, blue, and yellow swirled together in one massive bruise radiating out from the long, jagged scar that stretches across the length of the elbow. There are two black strings at either end of the scar, perfect little knots sticking up out of my mangled skin.

"Ugh," I breathe out, my face twisting up in disgust at the state of my arm. "It's worse than I pictured." I look away.

"It hasn't even been two weeks, yet, Nell," my mom reminds me. "It's going to take some time to heal and look normal again."

I risk one more look at it, then look away again, swallowing the bile that's creeping up my throat. If only my mom were right, if only I could be normal again.

Before my thoughts can spiral any further, the door opens and Dr. Sinclair enters, the same blonde nurse at his heels.

"Janelle," he starts, "so good to see you again. How're you feeling?" he asks, pulling a rolling stool over near the table and sitting down. The nurse hands him my chart and he flips through it, waiting for my answer.

"Okay, I guess," I tell him, not really sure what else to say. He looks up and gives me a genuine smile.

"Let's take a look," he says as he stands, holding my scans up to the display on the wall and sliding them up under the grooves into place. He looks from one to the next, quiet for a minute as he studies the black and white blobs.

"Well, it looks like things are healing nicely," he says, pointing to various parts of the blobs as if I know what's what. "Maybe a little too nicely," he adds, scratching the side of his nose.

"Uhh, okay?" I utter, unsure what he means.

"Your tendons and ligaments have fused themselves back in place where we want them," he explains, "they've just come back together a little tighter than I would have liked them."

"So my body basically overcorrected itself?" I ask.

"That's a good way of putting it," he nods. "Whereas before things were torn and loose, now they're tightening to the point where you might start to stiffen up and lose mobility."

My mom sits up taller in her chair at his words. "So she won't be able to move her arm anymore?" she questions, her voice cracking.

"Well, that would be an extreme case, but if we do nothing and let her body continue healing at this rate, then yes." He flicks the x-ray box off and comes back to the stool. "I'd like to propose a different course of treatment and physical therapy that should hopefully prevent that from happening."

"And what's that?" my mom asks.

"I'd like Janelle to start using an elbow continuous passive motion machine right away," he says.

"An elbow what machine?" I ask, panic creeping into my voice.

"Continuous passive motion," he repeats. "The CPM machine provides a specific type of range of motion therapy that allows your elbow to continuously move without any effort on your part," he says. He motions with his own arm, bending and straightening at the elbow, back and forth. "The machine does all the work. By keeping it moving, we'll prevent those tendons and ligaments from tightening up any further, and loosen things back out to where they should be. It's a somewhat cumbersome machine, but it yields great results."

I stare at him, unblinking. "So I'd just walk around with this thing strapped to my arm all day?" I ask him, afraid of what his answer will be.

"No," he chuckles, shaking his head at the thought. "You'd have to be at home. It can easily be installed next to your bed or couch, wherever you prefer. It should run whenever you're at rest."

"So I'd have to miss more school then?"

"I'm afraid so," he replies, confirming my fears. "For at least a month to start. Hopefully no longer than that. We can reevaluate then and see how you're doing."

My heart sinks into my stomach at the idea of another month at home. Staying home when Brendan wasn't speaking to me was appealing, but now that I have him back on my side, I don't want to miss any more school. Despite Shelley and Crystal blowing me off, and how painful it is seeing Jason with Bethany, I'd still rather be there with the guys to distract me than stuck at home by myself, with nothing but time to think about my mistakes and drown in my guilt.

I zone out as Dr. Sinclair continues discussing the machine and its protocols with my mom. I hear their voices as if I were underwater, distorted and muffled. All I can register is the sense of drowning I feel, my mind being pulled under by black, aching thoughts.

I only snap to when I feel a tug at my arm, and realize Dr. Sinclair is removing one long stitch from my arm. I feel it slide underneath my skin from one end only to pop out the other. I gag and resist the urge to vomit at the slippery feeling of the stitch pulling free of my body.

"You okay?" Dr. Sinclair asks, bringing me back to the present. He disposes of the stitch in a biohazard container by the sink.

"Mmmhmm," I gurgle.

"It's going to be alright, Janelle," he says reassuringly. "We'll plan to see you back here in a month, unless something comes up before then. Don't hesitate to call if you need anything."

He gives my shoulder a pat and stands to exit, my gaze following his shiny leather loafers as he moves out of the room.

*****

In the car on the ride home, I can't help looking over my shoulder every so often at the machine in the backseat. It looks high-tech and new, which makes me resent it even more.

"I know that wasn't what you were hoping to hear," my mom says, breaking the silence, "but you know it could be a lot worse. This is all temporary, at least. Just have to look on the bright side, Janelle." Her gaze is set firmly ahead on the road in front of us, her hands at ten and two on the wheel, but I can sense her frustration with me even without seeing it on her face.

I don't answer, afraid of what I might say to her.

"As for Florida," she continues, "there will be plenty of other chances to get there. Who knows, now that we're postponing, maybe Shelley will be able to join us after all. There's your silver lining, sweetie."

I clench my left hand into a fist, digging my nails into my palm so hard I can feel the skin split. "I don't give a flying turd about Florida, mom!" I finally crack, practically yelling. "The last thing I want is to be at the beach right now!" I slump further down in the seat, trying to inch away from her, closer to the window.

After the summer, I don't know that I ever want to be at the beach again.

She lets out a deep sigh through her nostrils but doesn't say any more the rest of the drive.

When we finally get home, my mom is silent as she carries the CPM machine into the house. I don't even bother to try and help, knowing I'd be useless anyway.

I make a beeline for the living room, kicking my Vans off as I walk through the house. As soon as I reach the safety of the couch, I dig my phone out of my pocket and flop down.

I hastily stab out a text to Brendan.

I feel like I'm spiraling. Can you come over tomorrow?

I hit send, bouncing my feet against the coffee table as I anxiously watch the screen for his reply.

What seems like a million minutes later, but really is only two minutes and eight seconds, I see the dots pop up on the screen, signaling his reply.

> Of course. I'll skip practice & come right after school. U gonna be okay til then?'

Yeah. Go to practice first. It's bad enough I'm not there these days. Those guys need you. Just come over after, I answer.

He sends back a heart emoji, but just like the last one he sent, it doesn't help calm the overwhelming stress building inside me.

At this point, without my good hand to wield something sharp, the only thing I can rely on right now is a strong helping of painkillers and the numbness that comes with it.

I grab for the Vicodin bottle on the table, dumping three pills into my palm and popping them into my mouth, washing them down with the half-empty glass of water on the table.

I try in vain not to count the seconds until sleep takes me.

Monday, October 25th
Fall of Freshman Year

The next afternoon, my mom seems to have forgotten our fight and is already right back in nagging mother mode, reminding me of my problems in a way she thinks is helpful.

"You really need to get back in the machine," she tells me. As if I've already forgotten Dr. Sinclair's diagnosis from yesterday.

"Brendan's coming over soon, can't I just take a little break?" I whine, trying to wear her down.

"I can't go round and round with you, Janelle," she says tiredly. "You have to want to help yourself, too. I can't force you. You heard Dr. Sinclair, it's going to take some time and effort on your part, but it will be worth it in the end. Come on, sweetie." Her voice softens and she gives me a sad smile, the fine lines around her eyes crinkling with the effort.

I sigh. “Fine.”

I adjust my posture on the couch, pushing my pillow away and scooting my butt all the way back so I’m sitting upright against the couch back. I gingerly lay my arm into the machine, the soft padding cushioning my skin as if sinking into a cloud.

My mom moves closer to help me tighten the straps to hold my arm in place. She double-checks everything to ensure it’s secure before flipping the power switch to *‘on.’* The machine makes a low humming sound as it forces my elbow to bend and straighten in slow, monotonous repetition.

Satisfied, my mom leans down and brushes my forehead with a kiss.

“I’m heading out to the barn, but I’ll have my phone with me. Just call if you need anything.”

“Brendan will be here soon, I’ll be fine until then,” I reply. “But thanks,” I add, trying to be a little nicer. I remind myself that even though this situation is the second worst thing I’ve ever been through, it isn’t her fault. She’s just trying to carry out the doctor’s orders. Although it definitely has been much easier being mad at her than at myself.

There's not much more guilt and shame I can handle at this point.

I watch her walk away, wishing I'd asked her to hand me the TV remote first. I let my eyes glaze over as a rerun of America's Next Top Model comes on, my eyelids getting heavy as my body relaxes. Since I've already seen this episode, I let my tired eyes close for just a minute while I wait for Brendan.

*****

"Nell? Hell-ooo, earth to Nell?"

My eyelids feel like lead as I pry them apart. Brendan is crouched in front of me, waving his hands in front of my face.

"Oh my god," I croak, smacking my lips and swallowing back the drool that's escaped my lips. "Sorry."

"No worries," he laughs as he backs away, settling into the La-Z-Boy. "You must be pretty beat. Although I can't imagine how you managed to fall asleep with that *thing* attached to you." He stares at the machine as it continues whirring, flexing my arm back and forth. "Things have certainly changed a bit since I saw you last," he continues, shaking his head and swishing his red hair out of his face. "And no pictures this time, promise," he adds, holding his hands up innocently.

"Thanks," I reply sheepishly, still feeling like an ass for blowing up at him. I rub the sleep out of my eyes with my left hand, wishing I didn't have to talk to Brendan while I'm sitting here like a living, breathing cyborg.

"So what's the deal with that thing, anyway?" he asks.

"Apparently my body is too good at healing," I explain.

If only my mind could heal as easily as my body.

"This will help loosen things back out," I continue explaining. "Otherwise, I'll lose mobility." I try to ignore the incessant back and forth of the machine, my right arm its hostage.

"How long do you have to be in it?"

"Pretty much all the time, for at least a month," I reply.

"Shit." His green eyes go wide and he puffs up his cheeks, pushing the air out in an exasperated sigh.

"Tell me about it," I agree as I roll my eyes.

"Well, we can't have you losing your mind stuck here by yourself, so I'll definitely come over all the time and keep you company. We can even get a few rounds of chess in here and there so you don't lose your touch. Although I wouldn't mind surpassing you as MVP," he says, cupping his chin, "So scratch that, maybe I won't help you stay sharp." He gives me a wicked grin and I laugh.

"Even with one hand, I'll always be better than you," I say and stick my tongue out at him. "So what'd I miss today? Any interesting news from the front lines?" I ask, eager for anything to take my mind off my problems.

"Nah, just the usual." He pauses for a minute, giving me a strange look. "Although," he continues, "You'll never believe who chased me down in the hallway today." He stares at me, waiting for me to ask.

"Who?" I finally question.

"That guy, Keith, you were talking to a while back."

My brow furrows, confused. "What? Why?" I ask. I think about the unanswered text from last week, wondering what he could possibly want from Brendan, especially considering how protective Brendan's been.

"He wanted me to give you this." Brendan reaches down into his backpack, resting against the side of his chair, and pulls out a folded piece of construction paper. He hands it over and I realize it's a Get Well card.

A handmade Get Well card.

The front of the card is decorated with a hand-drawn doodle of a sick whale, its tale wrapped in a bandage and a thermometer sticking out of its frowning mouth. I open the card and read the note Keith scrawled inside.

`Things can be over-whale-ming sometimes, but hang in there. Hope you get whale soon.`

I snort at the cheesy puns, then feel myself blush as I realize he signed it `xoxo Keith.`

I feel a mixed flutter of excitement and nervousness staring at those x's and oh's, struggling with the notion that he remembered my weird thoughts about receiving greeting cards. It's such a sweet gesture, but is it worth it to go down that road again? My mouth goes dry as I think about that kiss we shared at the top of my driveway. But then my stomach twists into knots as a different kiss creeps back into my head.

"What's his deal, anyway?" Brendan grunts, interrupting my thoughts just before they spiral completely out of control.

"What do you mean?" I ask. I set the card down on the coffee table.

"I thought you guys weren't a thing?" he says, bouncing his foot against the floor.

"We aren't. He's just being nice," I say. He looks at me like he doesn't believe me. "It's complicated," I add, knowing it's only *me* that's complicating everything.

He continues to stare at me for a beat, his silence unnerving.

"This is about Jason, isn't it?" he finally asks.

I try to find the words to reply, but he cuts me off.

"Why are you still so hung up on him, anyway? *You* dumped *him,* right?" His voice takes on a stern tone. "Just get over it and stop torturing yourself already." He pauses. "Stop torturing *me*." He crosses his arms and slumps back into the chair, refusing to look at me.

I open my mouth to say something, but I'm stunned into silence for a moment.

What does that even mean? I want to ask him.

"It's not that simple," I say instead, but he cuts me off before I can add anything else.

"God, Janelle. Why do you have to make everything so *complicated*? I can't take it anymore." His voice is barely a whisper and I wonder if we're still talking about Jason.

I heave a deep sigh at his use of the word complicated and look away, not sure how to react. I can feel his eyes boring into me as I avoid looking at him.

"I think I should go," he says finally.

"Yeah," I reply, gnawing the inside of my cheek as I continue to stare down at the floor.

I hear him move to get up, my eyes still trained on the hardwood.

"Things could be so much easier, y'know," he says before turning to leave, unaware of how further from the truth his words really are.

As he leaves, I hear him pull the front door shut quietly, which is even scarier than if he'd just slammed it in a rage on his way out. He thinks I'm over-complicating things, getting upset over nothing, that things could be so easy if I just let go of Jason and move on. That's easy for him to say, without knowing the truth, without having to live with the guilt and shame I've felt every day since that August night.

Nothing about this is easy.

Monday, August 6th
Summer Before Freshman Year

"Mom, come *on*," Janelle pleaded to Nora, after she'd washed up from her surf lesson. "It's *vacation*. How often will I get the chance to go to a bonfire on the beach?" she whined, trying to get her mother to cave.

"Janelle, I don't even know this boy. The answer is no," Nora replied, pulling her feet up into the hammock she was laying in and going back to her paperback.

"This is so unfair," Janelle grumbled as she slouched into one of the patio chairs. She picked at the peeling paint on the arm of the chair, staring daggers at her mom. The sliding door opened and her dad ambled out onto the pool deck.

"Woah, what's going on out here?" Darrell asked as he noticed the look on Janelle's face. "You could slice the tension in the air with a knife." He set a bag of chips and a bowl of salsa on the patio table and settled into the chair next to Janelle.

"Your daughter is just pouting because I told her she can't go out tonight."

"I'm not pouting," Janelle said. "I just don't understand why you won't let me have any fun on vacation."

"I'm not letting my 14-year-old-daughter go off to a party with some strange kid I've never met." Nora stood up from her hammock and came to the table. "End of discussion."

"There's going to be plenty of other kids there. What if Lauren goes with me?" Janelle asked.

"There's an idea," her dad interjected.

"Darrell, don't encourage her."

"What? I think Janelle's old enough to make her own decisions, and if Lauren goes, too, I don't see the problem." He shoveled a large bite of salsa into his mouth and shrugged.

Janelle gave her dad a grateful smile, then turned to her mother, pleadingly. "Pretty pretty please?" she begged.

Nora sighed. "Alright, fine. I give in. But only if Lauren goes with you."

Janelle got up from her chair and threw her arms around her mother. "Thanks mom," she told her. "You won't regret this."

Saturday, October 30th
Fall of Freshman Year

It's been four days, twenty hours, eleven minutes and two seconds since Brendan stormed out of my house. Although stormed doesn't feel like the right word. I wish he *had* stormed out, yelling and slamming the door. If he'd made a big scene, screaming at me in rage, then maybe by now things would have simmered down and we'd be talking again. Instead, he just slipped away into the night, making a silent exit from my house, and my life. Because unlike the last fight we had, I'm not sure how we come back from this one. If we even *can* come back from this.

Brendan called me complicated. Just like Shelley. And Keith. And who knows who else behind my back. And every single one of them was right, I *am* complicated, and everything I touch lately has turned to shit.

Brendan said things can be easy, but how do I pretend to be the carefree best friend he wants me to be? How can I be someone I'm not? How can I cover up the cracks in my facade and hide the darkness that oozes from me? The cracks grow wider every day and I worry eventually, they'll be so wide my insides will just spill out onto the floor, a puddle of Janelle for people to step over and around and pretend isn't there.

No one has said a word to me since Monday. Not Brendan, obviously. But not Dougie or Tyler, either. Shelley and Crystal are non-existent at this point, swallowed up by Bethany and Jason and their crew. Keith hasn't reached out since the get well card, which makes sense considering I never thanked him for it. There have been no calls, no texts, no tags on TikTok, no messages on Instagram, nothing from no one.

I try to ignore the fact that Halloween is tomorrow. That I should be getting my costume ready with my friends, not sitting here alone, in agony. And while, part of me knows I could just pick up the phone and fix this, another part of me knows I'll never *really* fix this whole mess that I got myself into in the first place. So why bother? It's easier to let my shame and self-pity pull me under and drown out everything else. Safer, too.

Between the lack of contact with the outside world, and the endless supply of Vicodin, the days blur together, a long, drawn-out version of the same miserable day on repeat. A twisted kind of Groundhog's Day. I wonder if this is how prisoners feel in solitary confinement.

My mom flutters around me like a hummingbird searching for nectar, tending to my needs the best she can, sighing and huffing at my lack of conversation and motivation. My dad's attempts at cheering me up are unending. He seems unaware that it will take more than a few lame jokes and goofy faces to crack a smile out of me, let alone a whole new personality. If he knew the secrets trapped inside me, he wouldn't try so hard to get me to interact.

My arm continues to move independent of my body, the machine pushing it back and forth, up and down, endlessly straightening and bending, refusing to stop, refusing to let things have a moment to seize up. I wish there was a machine to stretch out the knots tangled up in my stomach, another one to clear away the murky thoughts swirling in my mind. If only a machine could fix the source of my true pain.

Since Brendan left me, I've felt a shift. I no longer yearn for the comfort of my safety pins, the weight of a paper clip held between my fingertips, the smooth, cold metal of scissors pressed into my palms. I no longer wish for the sweet release that comes with sliding the sharp edge of a blade against my skin. I knew all along I was just trading one pain for another, exchanging the emotional agony for a physical one. But I realize now it wasn't enough. In the end, the ache remained, the uneasiness lingered, the guilt still wormed its way through my veins no matter how hard I tried to let it out.

As the days pile on, the more pills I have to take just to feel nothing. The numbness takes longer to sink in, wears away too quickly. A temporary fix for a never-ending problem. It, too, becomes not enough, because I know it, like all else, will abandon me, leave me wanting more, leave me unsatisfied. My thoughts have become consumed with finding a permanent fix, a solution to stop the suffocating guilt, the shame that squeezes my chest tight like a vise until I can no longer breathe.

I can feel a solution on the tip of my tongue, begging to be said.

A way out.

An escape from the pain.

I feel it building a little more each day, the words getting closer and closer to slipping from my mouth. I let them whisper through my bones, shuffling into coherent thought, rearranging to fit perfectly together into the answer. I just have to be patient and wait.

Soon, I will feel nothing.

Tuesday, November 2nd
Fall of Freshman Year

As I stare at the almost-full bottle of Vicodin my mom refilled yesterday, my answer begins to take shape in my mind. Slow at first, but growing the more I let my brain wrap around it, until I can see it clear as day.

I grab the bottle and unscrew the cap, tipping several pills into my hand.

I line them up in a row on the coffee table, one for each friendship I've ruined, for each problem I've created with this mess I've made.

Jason. Bethany. Shelley. Crystal. Keith. Tyler. Dougie. Brendan.

Travis.

His name hovers on the tip of my tongue, begging to be said. It's been there this whole time, lurking at the edge of my darkest thoughts, waiting to pull me under.

So I let it.

I dump the remaining pills out onto the table, letting my plan sharpen into focus, knowing that everything leads back to Travis, and that night, and what we did. The catalyst for all of this.

How differently my life would look right now if it wasn't for that one wrong summer.

Monday, August 6th
Summer Before Freshman Year

"Ugh, are we almost there?" Lauren whined as she clomped through the sand and dirt behind Janelle, swatting at the sea oats that blew into their path.

"Should be just up ahead," Janelle replied, shining her phone's flashlight on the trail down to the beach. She walked a few more paces ahead of her sister before she broke through the tall grass and out onto the flat sand.

"There!" she cried excitedly as she spotted a group of people hovering near a crackling fire.

Janelle grabbed her sister's hand and dragged her along the smooth beach towards the party. As they got closer, they could hear laughter and the thumping of music from someone's phone. There were a few kids sitting on a large tree that had fallen horizontal in the sand; others stood around the fire, and several more hovered near a silver keg. Everyone held red, shiny Solo cups.

The bonfire flickered haphazardly, throwing warped shadows over everything, making it hard to see what was going on all at once. Janelle scanned the crowd, searching for Travis's blonde hair and blue eyes in every face. Finally, she spotted him off to the side of the fire, talking with another blonde-haired guy. She dragged her sister by the hand as she shuffled through the sand towards him.

"Hey." She tried to make her voice sound sultry and seductive but it came out hoarse instead. She cleared her throat to calm her nerves, dropping Lauren's hand and giving him a small wave as he turned to face her.

"Hey, you made it," he smiled, and leaned in for a hug, breathing in the coconut shampoo in her hair. She nuzzled against his shirt.

"Ehem," Lauren interrupted, and Janelle pulled away from Travis. "I'm her sister, Lauren," she informed him, crossing her arms and taking a step toward Travis, forcing him to back up.

"Hey, Lauren," Travis said with a sly smile. "Welcome. Here, let's get you girls a drink." He gestured towards his friend, who was still lingering next to him. "Benji? You mind?" Travis gave Benji a look, who returned it with a slight nod, passing his cup to Travis.

"We're good, thanks," Lauren interjected before Travis could hand off the drinks. Janelle turned to her sister, glaring daggers through the darkness and into the side of her face. She grabbed Lauren's hand and pulled her closer.

"Don't make me look bad," Janelle grumbled at her sister through gritted teeth.

"We're not drinking," Lauren whispered back at her. "That wasn't part of the deal."

"Just take the damn cup and don't be lame," Janelle seethed, willing her sister to just play along and be cool for once in her life.

"*Fine*," Lauren ceded. She turned to the guys. "We'd love a drink," she said, giving them a big, fake smile.

Travis passed Benji's cup to Janelle. "You guys can go get a fresh one," he said to Lauren. Benji held out his hand to the older sister, but she just looked at it disgustedly, so he let it drop back to his side. She did take a few steps toward him, though, so he held out his hand very gentleman-like, palm up, to motion her ahead of him.

"I have a boyfriend, you know," Lauren told Benji as she moved away with him towards the keg. "And so does she," she added, turning back to Travis and tilting her chin at her sister before turning her back to them.

Janelle clenched her fists, digging her nails into her palms as she watched Lauren walk off.

"She seems...*nice*," Travis snorted and took a gulp of his drink.

"Yeah," was all Janelle could come up with as a reply. She gripped her cup with both hands and watched as Travis took another big swig from his own. Hesitantly, Janelle put her lips to the rim of the cup, tipping it up slightly to allow the cool liquid to reach her mouth. It was frothy and smelled like citrus; she parted her lips away from the rim ever so slightly and let the smallest bit slip past her lips and down her throat. It felt refreshing as she swallowed, but the bitter aftertaste made her scrunch up her face in disgust.

"You get used to it," Travis chuckled at her.

Janelle gave him a closed-mouth smile, unsure she *wanted* to get used to it, but she took another sip anyway.

"You wanna chill?" Travis asked, gesturing to a spot on the end of the fallen tree two girls had just vacated.

"Sure," Janelle replied. She took another sip of her drink, this one bigger than the last, as Travis reached over and took her hand in his. His grip was firm, but his skin felt soft and smooth against hers. Her stomach did a somersault, but she wasn't sure if it was nerves or excitement or a little of both.

He led her to the tree and motioned for her to sit. Janelle perched on the edge, her knees pressed together and heels up against the side of the log, steadying herself. Travis plunked down next to her and scooted closer, his legs angled in towards her so his knees were touching hers. Janelle cradled her cup in her lap and stared out at the fire blazing before them.

"This is cool," she said. She scrambled to find something more interesting to say, but nothing came to mind, so she took a gulp of her drink instead. She peered down into the cup, not realizing she'd already drank more than half of what was mostly a full cup to start.

"Yeah," Travis answered, watching her watch the fire. "Bunch of us get together a couple times a month and do this. It's sort of a townie thing, no tourists allowed, but we had such a good time earlier, I figured, why not keep having fun together? No one has to know."

At that, Janelle glanced over at Travis and met his gaze. The blue of his eyes mixed with the reflection of the flames made his eyes look like they were glittering. She didn't realize she was staring until he reached over and stroked her cheek, his thumb tracing the edge of her mouth.

"Janelle." At the sound of Lauren's voice, Janelle jumped, pulling away from Travis. Her sister was hovering over her, Benji coming up next to her. He slung his arm around Lauren's shoulder but she shrugged it off, repulsed.

"Hey, you get a drink?" Janelle asked, trying to sound casual, but her words were already starting to slur together. She commanded her brain to focus, unwilling to be so obvious that this was her first time drinking.

"No," Lauren started, "but it sounds like *you've* had plenty. C'mon, we're going." She put her hand out for Janelle to take, but Janelle just swatted it away.

"Okay, *mom*," she huffed, drawing chuckles from both boys. "We're just having a little fun, ever heard of it?" She tipped her head back and downed the remainder of her drink, smacking her lips together in satisfaction and tossing the empty cup playfully at her sister.

"Real nice," Lauren retorted. She crossed her arms over her chest. "Now get up, we're leaving."

"I'm not ready to leave," Janelle replied.

"Janelle." Lauren reached down to grab her sister's arm.

"No!" Janelle practically yelled, yanking her arm away from her sister and almost tumbling off the back of the log. Travis put his arm out to steady her back into an upright position.

"Stop making a fool of yourself and let's go," Lauren hissed through a clenched jaw.

"Hey, she said she's not ready to leave," Travis interjected.

"Who even *are* you?" Lauren turned, glaring down at him. "Just stay out of this."

"I'm not going. You can't make me." Now it was Janelle's turn to cross her arms.

"Are you serious right now?" Lauren asked. "Fine, then I'm telling mom."

"Go 'head," Janelle replied, waving her sister away wildly with both arms.

Lauren stomped off, leaving Janelle, Travis, and Benji giggling like small children.

"What a drama queen," Benji said.

"For sure," Travis nodded, taking a sip of his drink. "We'll have more fun without her," he assured Janelle, patting her knee, his hand lingering behind on her bare skin.

"Totally," she agreed, not entirely convinced. As she looked off in the direction her sister had gone, wondering if she should have just gone with her, Janelle didn't notice Benji dumping something white and powdery into his cup.

"Another drink?" Travis asked her, drawing her attention back. He looked up at Benji, who gave him a knowing nod, swishing the liquid in his cup before passing it over. Then he slunk away towards a group of people on the other end of the log, leaving them alone. Travis set the cup in Janelle's lap and wrapped her hands around it, then cupped her chin with his hand and pulled her gaze back towards him.

Feeling more than a little buzzed, Janelle blinked her eyes a few times to try and clear the fog settling into her brain. How many drinks had she had so far? She thought it was only one, but she couldn't remember.

She looked up into Travis's eyes and everyone else seemed to fade into the background. He pulled her face close to his and ducked down to kiss her, deep and long. She finally pulled away for a breath, feeling lightheaded, although she couldn't tell if it was from the kiss or something else. She let out an unexpected giggle and sighed.

Travis leaned in close, brushing his lips against her ear, his breath hot on her skin.

"I want to show you something," he whispered.

Thursday, November 4th
Fall of Freshman Year

I've come to terms with my decision. Once it came to me, how easily I embraced it. If only I'd thought of it sooner.

I count the days, the hours, the minutes, the seconds until I'll be well on my way to escaping for good. Two days, eight hours, sixteen minutes and four seconds.

Three months exactly.

I feel a sense of calm wash over me as time ticks by, hurtling me closer to the end. Any unease, any anxiety, any fear I might have felt has fallen away.

I'm closer and closer to feeling nothing.

I wonder if I should leave a note, a sign, some sort of farewell for anyone who might be looking for it. Not that anyone would be. I haven't communicated with anyone in ten days, one hour, eleven minutes and nine seconds. I doubt anyone even remembers my name.

After days in self-isolation, I turn my phone back on and pull open Instagram, deciding I'll leave a cryptic message for anyone willing to decipher my code, anyone worthy enough to put in the time. Although it will be too little too late by the time they figure it out.

As my phone boots up, my notifications explode, my inbox bursting with unread text messages. I recognize some names and numbers, but not all.

I open the most recent one in the list, a group thread from Will.

I kno it's kinda last min, but planning 2 hold Eddie's memorial Sat am. Lemme kno who can make it, if any1 can help w/ setup, etc

I do a double-take, rereading Will's message to the rest of the chess team. Eddie's memorial? *What*?

I open a few more messages, scanning them quickly before swiping back to my newsfeed. I scroll through countless posts from friends and acquaintances, all pictures of Eddie Langley's smiling face, all the captions saying similar things.

RIP Eddie.

We miss you.

Gone too soon.

I close Instagram and do a quick Google search. Within seconds, the search results pull up the local paper's article on the deadly crash that happened three days ago on Winding Creek Road, two miles from school. I skim the article, taking away the meat of the story. Eddie was driving home from school, speeding around the twists and turns Winding Creek is known for, when he lost control of the car and smashed into a tree. He was the only person in the car, and no others were involved. A passing car stopped and called 911. Eddie was already dead when the EMTs arrived.

Eddie died.

Eddie's dead.

The words sink in and I realize the weight they carry. I'll never again play him in chess, never again smile to myself as I watch him across the board, his nose twitching with concentration, trying hard to beat me. I'll never again hear his laugh, hearty and deep, as he tells his famous jokes to keep us entertained on long bus rides to competitions. I won't have to worry anymore about what I say around him, wondering if my private conversations will make it back to Jason like they did last time.

But I'd take a million versions of that blowup at lunch if it meant Eddie was still alive.

As I cycle through the harsh reality of Eddie's death, I feel bile rising in my throat. I gag, swallowing it back down. I can feel sweat beading at my temples, at the edge of my hairline. My eyes blur and I feel dizzy.

I swipe out of Google and pull up my phone's keypad, tapping at the screen, stabbing with my finger until Brendan's number comes up. His cell rings twice before he answers, but I barely let him say hello before I start blubbering into the phone.

"I know you hate me right now. I hate me too. But I really need you."

I pause, trying to find my breath.

"Please, hurry."

Monday, August 6th
Summer Before Freshman Year

Travis stood from the log and reached down to help Janelle up. Standing so quickly sent a rush to her head, and she fell into Travis's broad chest. He slipped an arm around her shoulder to steady her and helped her away from the bonfire and the others. She stumbled along in the sand, leaning into Travis to keep herself upright.

As they passed the group Benji was talking to, the two boys locked eyes for a moment and exchanged a look before Travis steered Janelle away, down the beach towards the water.

When they got to the shoreline, Janelle perked up slightly at the loud crashing of the waves, getting her balance back a bit, but she was still finding it hard to keep her eyes open.

"Here," Travis said, letting go of Janelle momentarily to take off his t-shirt and lay it on the sand at the water's edge. He sat down and reached up to help her. She took his hands and crumpled into him, giggling again as he caught her before she rolled into the sand.

"'S nice here," Janelle slurred, letting her eyes close for a minute as she leaned into Travis.

"Beautiful, isn't it?" he replied. "Just like you." He pulled her face up to his and kissed her again, and she let herself just relax and enjoy it, keeping her eyes closed. This time, when she tried to pull away and come up for air, Travis just pressed his mouth harder against hers. Finally, she managed to pull free, leaning away from him slightly as she tried to shake her head clear again.

"I have a boyfriend, 'member?" she said, her voice barely a whisper.

"I know," Travis replied, "but he's not here, is he?" Travis grabbed her face again and forced his lips to hers.

She tried to pull away again, even tried to push him back, but she could feel herself getting weaker the more she tried, and it only seemed to spur him on. Instead of letting up, he forced his hand up her shirt and pushed her down into the sand.

"We can't," she mumbled, but those words didn't seem right. She tried to force her brain to cooperate with her tongue but her head still felt fuzzy and she couldn't figure out the right way to make this stop, how to make him stop.

"It's okay," he whispered into her hair, mashing his mouth against her neck.

"No," Janelle murmured, shaking her head slowly back and forth in the sand. "No. Stop. I made a mistake." The words stuck to her tongue like molasses, yielding no results.

She could hear him grunting over her now, his hot breath stale with beer every time he exhaled into her face. She wanted to push him off, push him away, but her arms felt like lead and she could barely lift them.

She kept shaking her head, whispering "*no*" over and over, but he wouldn't stop. She could feel the urge to scream deep down inside her, but she couldn't find the energy to cry out.

Instead, she closed her eyes and started counting the seconds until it was over.

One, two, three, four, five...

*****

"God, you're so beautiful," Travis whispered in her ear what felt like hours later, but was really just four minutes and twelve seconds. Janelle knew, because she had counted every single second.

She shuddered at his words, words that were supposed to make her feel happy and alive. All the times Jason had ever told her she was beautiful, when he'd smile at her across the table at dinner, or when he'd hold her hand walking down the street, all those times she felt giddy with satisfaction, glad to be wanted. Those words were supposed to make her feel safe and loved, but coming out of Travis's mouth, they just made her feel dirty and used.

"I should probably get home," Janelle croaked as she finally found her voice, the fog slowly lifting from her brain. She wobbled her way up to sitting, putting her hands out in the sand for support.

"Okay," Travis replied, standing up. "C'mon, I'll take you."

He reached a hand down to Janelle. She wanted to run from him, to get as far away from him as possible, but she still felt dizzy and knew there was no way she could make it back on her own. She grabbed his hand nervously, and let him help her to her feet.

Travis steered Janelle back up the beach and past the bonfire, where a smaller group of people were still laughing and drinking and carrying on. She half-hoped to see her sister's face in the crowd, but she didn't, nor did she see the blonde friend of

Travis's. The faces were all unrecognizable, and no one even looked their way as they passed.

When they got to the beach parking lot, Travis hoisted Janelle up into the cab of his pickup. She slid her seatbelt into place and slumped against the seat, fighting back tears as Travis let himself into the driver's side and revved the engine.

"Where to?" he asked her.

It took her a minute to remember the address where she was staying, the house where her parents was probably fast asleep, oblivious to what their younger daughter was up to.

She mumbled a street address and Travis took off into the night. As the dark shapes of houses whirred past, Janelle kept her focus out the window, refusing to look at the guy who just took her virginity.

"That was fun," Travis said as he shifted the truck into park on the street in front of her house. "But you probably shouldn't tell anyone what we did. After all, what would your boyfriend think?" He turned to Janelle, giving her a look that was part pity, part threat.

She gulped back a sob and instead gave him a small nod. Janelle felt a small jolt of relief when Travis made no move to get out of the truck and help her down. Eager to get away from him, she pushed the passenger door open quickly, shutting it quietly in hopes no one would suddenly wake and see her fleeing his truck.

As she stepped back onto the sidewalk, Travis peeled away into the night, leaving Janelle standing there, alone and devastated over what they'd done. She turned towards the house, already thinking through the text she'd have to send when the sun came up.

Thursday, November 4th
Fall of Freshman Year

By the time I'm done recounting that last night on the beach with Travis, I'm no longer crying, just hiccupping and sniffling back the snot that keeps threatening to slide down my face. I wipe at my eyes to clear any lingering tears and risk a sideways glance at Brendan. His hands are clasped to his mouth and his face is solemn, his gaze staring off. He takes a deep breath before he finally looks over at me, dropping his hands.

"You haven't told anyone this whole time?" he asks.

"How could I?" I say. "I'm so ashamed of what I've done. If anyone knew... God, if *Jason* knew what I did..." I drop my gaze to my feet, unable to go on.

"What *you* did? Janelle, what happened," he starts, searching for his next words, struggling to look at me, "what he did to you...you know that was... *rape*, right?" He has a pained look on his face as he exhales the words.

"No," I shake my head, too embarrassed to make eye contact. "No, it's my fault. I shouldn't have gone there that night, I shouldn't have kissed him, I shouldn't have led him on like that." I keep shaking my head, trying to shake away the memory of that night. "I shouldn't have let it happen."

"You didn't ask for that, Nell. That wasn't your fault." He pauses and waits for me to look up. "You have to stop blaming yourself."

His green eyes have softened, but I don't see pity in them, just sadness.

Hearing him say it out loud, it suddenly hits me.

All this time, blaming myself, thinking that I got what I asked for.

I never asked for any of this.

I said no.

How could I have spent all this time thinking it was my fault? Punishing myself for what he did.

It hits me like a wave all at once, but I suddenly feel like a fog has lifted. As the realization sinks in, I feel my guilt begin to melt away, slowly, bit by bit. I nod, not trusting myself to speak for fear of sobbing again.

"And what you said before," he continues, "when you called. Nothing you could ever do would make me hate you. Ever." He reaches over and takes my left hand in both of his, squeezing it gently. "I'll always be here for you."

"Promise?" I ask him nervously.

"Promise," he says, still holding my hand. He stares intently into my eyes.

I break eye contact and pull away, pausing for a moment to take a breath before finally pushing up the left sleeve of my shirt to expose the cuts and scars there.

When I meet his gaze again, he's biting his lower lip, a grimace on his face. His eyes look wet with tears, although whether they're sad tears or angry tears, I can't quite tell.

"I can't be like this anymore," I blubber, my nose dripping again. "I don't want it to get to the point where I... I was gonna... " I trail off, sick at the thought of saying what I'd almost done, what I was planning. My body shakes as I choke back sobs.

"Oh, Janelle," Brendan murmurs, and pulls me into a tight hug.

I let myself cry into his shoulder, my tears and snot leaking onto his shirt, absorbing there as a reminder of all that I'm letting go of. In that moment, with Brendan's arms around me, I no longer feel hopeless. I no longer feel like I have to run, have to escape.

Instead, I feel comforted knowing I'm no longer the only one carrying my secrets. All the shame and regret I've been burdened with these last several months slowly begins to fade away, and in their place, I feel something like relief.

Saturday, November 13th
Fall of Freshman Year

I'm sitting on the porch swing, pushing myself back and forth as I watch the road, waiting for Brendan to arrive. I check my watch and see I still have five minutes and four seconds until he said he would pick me up. While I wait, I pull my phone from my pocket and scroll back through my texts to Jason, hovering over our last conversation from August.

I can't do this anymore.

What do u mean? Can't do what?

I don't want to be your girlfriend anymore.

Nell pick up the phone

Plz

Don't do this

Nell?

Plz answer me

Nell pick up the phone

It's over. Please just accept that.

What happened? What did I do?

I just don't want to be with you anymore. Just move on.

Nell plz

We can fix this

Just tell me what I did wrong

I read the string of texts one more time, burning them into my memory before swiping left and deleting the conversation history.

The sadness I still feel about losing Jason lingers, but each day I feel a little stronger, a little more at peace with everything that happened. One day, I'll tell him the real story of why we broke up, but for today, I just feel lucky to be alive.

When Brendan finally pulls up to the house, I can hear the classic rock station blaring from the speakers of his 2008 Toyota Corolla. As I make my way up the driveway towards the car, the lines of Queen's *Bohemian Rhapsody* become clearer and clearer the closer I get, Freddie Mercury belting out the words as if his life depended on it. Which, I guess according to the lyrics, it did. I feel a shiver wash over me as I listen to the words, realizing how much truth there is in them, especially the line about not wanting to die.

It takes hearing a song through the crackly speakers of a beat-up old car to realize that I never really wanted that. It was only a last resort. But as I yank the passenger door open and slide onto the cracked leather seat next to Brendan, I realize I have another way out.

"Hey," I squeak as I settle in.

"Hey," Brendan replies, turning the knob on the radio to lower the volume.

"Thanks again for doing this," I mumble, feeling nervous and uncomfortable around my best friend for the first time.

"Of course. Anything for you, Nell," he replies. "Although you really should tell your parents." He gives me a small, sad smile in what I assume is an attempt to be helpful without pushing me too much. I return with a half-smile and click my seatbelt.

"Soon," I say, and he nods, shifting the car into drive and taking off.

*****

At 12:57 pm, Brendan rolls the car to a stop in front of a weathered-looking building. The parking lot is half full, 13 empty cars parked neatly in their rows. Guess we weren't as early as I hoped we'd be. He shifts the car to park, then turns to me, squeezing my left hand with his right.

"You got this, Nell. I'll be right outside when you're done. Provided I don't get busted for driving on a permit." He grins at me, an attempt at some humor to lighten the mood.

I give him a small smile back, grateful he's still the same ol' Brendan, even after everything that's happened, everything I've told him. I squeeze his hand back, letting it go as I push open the passenger door and step gingerly out into the hazy sunlight.

I move at a quick shuffle toward the front door. There's an older guy scrolling on his phone as he smokes a cigarette on the sidewalk. I brave a quick glance at him as I pass; he gives me a knowing nod.

With my good arm, I pull the door, squinting as my eyes adjust to the change in lighting. I pull a scrap of paper from my pocket: *Room 101A, down the hallway, make a left*, Brendan's scribbled handwriting reads.

I take a few hesitant steps down the hall, breathing in and out through my nose. When the hallway splits, I turn left, coming up on room 101A almost immediately. The door has one of those half windows you see on classroom doors; I spot several people inside seated in a circle of folding chairs, a few milling about at a table of snacks. I take one final breath and push open the door. A few people look up as I enter, welcoming me with their sad eyes and small smiles. I take an empty seat between a woman in a black dress and a boy in ripped jeans. They both give me a quick, courteous nod.

"Welcome," the woman smiles at me. I meet her eyes and shyly smile back.

An older man in a white button-up walks over from the snack table, taking a chair on the other side of the woman in the black dress. He claps his hands together and smiles at the group.

"Welcome back, everyone. I see we have a few new faces with us this week. Let's start by meeting our newcomers, shall we?" He turns to me with an earnest look, but somehow I don't feel nervous. He puts out his hand and gestures for me to stand, so I do. I look around the circle at all the faces watching me.

There are several women, and a few girls, but also a few men, and the boy with the ripped jeans. They're all waiting for me to speak. I clear my throat.

"Hi. My name is Janelle. I'm a victim--," I pause, shake my head to clear it. "Um, I mean, I'm a *survivor* of sexual violence." It takes me a moment to get the words out, and I bite my lip, unsure if I've said the right thing or not, but everyone's kind faces tell me I have.

"Hi, Janelle," they sing back in unison.

I sit back down as the next person stands, a small smile creeping across my face, a weight lifted.

AFTERWORD

While Janelle's experiences are fictionalized, they happen all too often in real life. Please know you are not alone, and there are many resources available should you need them.

National Suicide Prevention Lifeline:
1-800-273-TALK (8255)

Rape, Abuse, & Incest National Network:
1-800-656-HOPE (4673)

National Drug & Alcohol Treatment:
1-800-662-HELP (4357)

ACKNOWLEDGMENTS

Thank you to my husband, for supporting me no matter what, and for making a beautiful cover to accompany this story. Thank you to my friends and family, for cheering me on every step of the way. And thank you to every reader who believed in this story and saw it through to the end. I'm so grateful to have the opportunity to put words down on the page and bring them to life for others to enjoy.

P.S. If you enjoyed One Wrong Summer, please consider leaving a review wherever possible (Amazon, Goodreads, Instagram, etc.), as it creates more visibility and allows more readers to discover the story. Thank you for supporting indie authors!

ABOUT THE AUTHOR

Julia Bodwell is an educator, writer, and musician living in Florida with her husband and their rescue cat. She's obsessed with Halloween and summertime and loves to curl up with a good book as often as possible. *One Wrong Summer* is her first novel.

Visit her at juliabodwell.com to subscribe to her newsletter. Follow her @jbodwellwrites on social media to stay in touch.

Made in the USA
Middletown, DE
03 August 2022

70276532R00176